Easing the silent Beretta from its sheath, the Executioner moved cautiously down the dark and lifeless street. As he walked, he was reminded of the climactic showdown in *High Noon*. The tall silent stranger with a gun, stalking his villainous prey as he fought to "clean up the town." Bolan did not overlook the apt simile between that mythical crusade and his own grim war without end.

He paced the street—every sense on the alert for danger. His slim Beretta nosed out ahead of him like a sensor of peril. Bolan was ready.

A dark man-shape filled one of the empty doorways, and faint starlight gleamed on polished gun metal as the man brought his heavy automatic to bear on Bolan. The Beretta got there first, sneezing out a pair of silent words to discourage the foe. The deadly slugs sighed in on target, punching twin paths through headbone barely a finger's width apart. The human silhouette dematerialized, leaving the doorway empty again in the night.

Mafia. Bolan knew it with certainty. The guy had been on nightwatch, in the wrong place at the wrong time. His tab had come due to the universe for past wrongs inflicted, and the bill had been collected in full. That was the end of it. But not for Bolan . . .

Also by Don Pendleton

THE EXECUTIONER: MIAMI MASSACRE
THE EXECUTIONER: ASSAULT ON SOHO
THE EXECUTIONER: CHICAGO WIPEOUT
THE EXECUTIONER: VEGAS VENDETTA
THE EXECUTIONER: CARIBBEAN KILL
THE EXECUTIONER: CALIFORNIA HIT
THE EXECUTIONER: BOSTON BLITZ
THE EXECUTIONER: WASHINGTON I.O.U.
THE EXECUTIONER: SAN DIEGO SIEGE
THE EXECUTIONER: PANIC ON PHILLY
THE EXECUTIONER: NIGHTMARE IN NEW YORK
THE EXECUTIONER: JERSEY GUNS
THE EXECUTIONER: TEXAS STORM
THE EXECUTIONER: DETROIT DEATHWATCH
THE EXECUTIONER: NEW ORLEANS KNOCKOUT
THE EXECUTIONER: FIREBASE SEATTLE
THE EXECUTIONER: HAWAIIAN HELLGROUND
THE EXECUTIONER: ST LOUIS SHOWDOWN
THE EXECUTIONER: CANADIAN CRISIS
THE EXECUTIONER: COLORADO KILL-ZONE
THE EXECUTIONER: ACAPULCO RAMPAGE
THE EXECUTIONER: SAVAGE FIRE
THE EXECUTIONER: COMMAND STRIKE
THE EXECUTIONER: CLEVELAND PIPELINE

and published by Corgi Books

Don Pendleton

Executioner 31:
ARIZONA AMBUSH

CORGI BOOKS
A DIVISION OF TRANSWORLD PUBLISHERS LTD

EXECUTIONER 31: ARIZONA AMBUSH
A CORGI BOOK 0 552 10830 8

PRINTING HISTORY
Corgi edition published 1978

Corgi Books are published by Transworld Publishers Ltd
Century House, 61-63 Uxbridge Road,
Ealing, London, W.5.
Made and printed in Great Britain by
William Collins Sons & Co. Ltd., Glasgow

To the memory of Don Bolles,
a journalistic soldier of the
same side, who fell in the real
battle for Arizona (still in progress).
He died as he lived: largely,
with great waves.
Let it be not in vain.

DP

Special thanks to Mike Newton
for valuable assistance in the development
of this book.

"Man is that part of reality in which and through which the cosmic process has become conscious and has begun to comprehend itself. His supreme task is to increase that conscious comprehension and to apply it as fully as possible to guide the course of events . . . to discover his destiny as agent of the evolutionary process. . . ."

—JULIAN HUXLEY

"I have only one purpose, the destruction of Hitler, and my life is much simplified thereby."

—WINSTON CHURCHILL

"There is little comfort in a life dedicated to thunderation and hellfire everlasting. But I accept the role destiny has handed me. The goals then become simplified. I live only for the destruction of the Mafia."

—MACK BOLAN, from his journal

CONTENTS

	Prologue	1
Chapter 1	Solutions	5
Chapter 2	Jokers	14
Chapter 3	Paradise	20
Chapter 4	Pros	28
Chapter 5	Understandings	37
Chapter 6	Connections	46
Chapter 7	Convincers	56
Chapter 8	The Wedge	63
Chapter 9	Sucking	71
Chapter 10	Audacity	79
Chapter 11	The Message	88
Chapter 12	Symbols	96
Chapter 13	Face	108
Chapter 14	Links	118
Chapter 15	One More Time	126
Chapter 16	Hearts	133
Chapter 17	Rift	141
Chapter 18	Pawns Out	148
Chapter 19	Score	154
Chapter 20	Fragged	159
Chapter 21	Bagged	166
	Epilogue	175

ARIZONA
AMBUSH

PROLOGUE

Personal awakening may come in many forms, the variations as infinite as the possibilities of human development. For young Sergeant Mack Bolan, that awakening came one summer afternoon in the form of a telegram. Bolan was completing his second combat tour of duty in South Vietnam when word reached him of the deaths of his father, mother, and sister. Returning to the States to care for those beloved dead, Bolan had been thrust jarringly into head-on confrontation with a shady underside of civilization that most people never see or even imagine.

Mack Bolan's family had run afoul of the Mafia, that sinister criminal society which had blossomed from its own tiny beginnings a century ago into what one recent attorney general called the "invisible second government" of the United

States, with bloody hands dipping into virtually every legal or illicit field of enterprise imaginable.

A highly skilled professional warrior, Mack Bolan early recognized the means by which the evil *mafiosi* have managed to frustrate and emasculate the American legal system, and he reacted in the only way remaining. It was a technique which, in Vietnam, had earned him the label of The Executioner.

"What's the use in fighting an enemy 8,000 miles away," young Bolan had asked, "when the *real* enemy is tearing up everything you love back home?" Thus was the Executioner's war brought to America, an unending holy war against the forces of evil, the forces of Mafia. Against all the odds, the warrior survived his first engagement with the omnipotent crime syndicate and swept on to confront the brutal godfathers on other battlefields. Wherever La Cosa Nostra reared its foul head, the implacable Executioner was ready, willing, and able to lop off that head.

The Mafia was taken totally off guard, woefully unprepared to face Mack Bolan's personal style of relentless warfare. They knew that in the end they must win out, the odds were simply *too* great, *too* impossible for any one man, even a supremely conditioned warrior, to stand indefinitely against the combined might of the organization. And yet, in the meantime, Bolan seemed to lead a charmed life as he rampaged across the Mafia's fortress America at will, pillaging the empire of corruption and evil.

The Executioner's latest foray against the syndicate legions had been in Cleveland, Ohio, where he frustrated the imperial dreams of one Bad

Tony Morello and routed the Mafia troops again. It was Bolan's thirtieth campaign against the mob, and even the soldier himself realized that his string of good fortune could not last forever. It would run out one day, probably sooner than later. But in the meantime, Bolan was determined to use the last ounce of his strength—the last drop of his life's blood—to carry out his war against the enemy. His was a war without quarter asked or given, a war without possibility of peace or surrender, short of the grave.

A Marine captain,* in a different war for similar, if not identical, goals, had written a hymn to gallantry in battle which well characterized Bolan's quixotic quest:

> *Who plows the sky, said a wise man,*
> *Shows himself a fool;*
> *But he went out to plow it—*
> *Taught in a different school.*
> *Who sows the wind, says Scripture,*
> *Must reap and reap again;*
> *But he went out to sow the wind—*
> *And reaped the bitter grain.*
> *He took his death like charity,*
> *Like nothing understood;*
> *He freshened all the oldest words*
> *With all his blood.*

Yeah, Executioner Mack Bolan was ready and willing to spend his blood, and that of his enemies, to freshen those old words. Words like peace, justice, virtue. Words with meaning even

* Richard G. Hubler: "Song for a Pilot"

3

yet, although the Mafia had done its level best to distort and erase that meaning.

The Executioner was prepared to put the meaning back into those hallowed words.

With all his blood.

CHAPTER 1

SOLUTIONS

The big man crouched in darkness, immobile, his alert senses sending out reconnaissance probes into the surrounding blackness. Around him, the desert was vibrantly alive with secret movement—the nocturnal thrust and counterthrust of instinctive survival. Insects trilled lightly in the thorny bush beside the man, and somewhere on his flank a sidewinder lisped across the sand in its endless search for prey. The man, Mack Bolan, was also hunting, but his quarry was far deadlier than the venomous desert reptile.

The Executioner was hunting cannibals. He had followed their spoor from the killing grounds in Cleveland to the arid expanses of Arizona, where he found them in abundance. The Mafia savages were there, daily strengthening their parasitic grip upon society in the Grand Canyon State. There had, indeed, been such a wealth of targets that Bolan spent the better part of a week in Tucson merely cataloguing them and gauging their numbers, seeking the most propitious point and moment to strike. Amid the now familiar recital of scams and swindles which everywhere marked the symptoms of the Mafia cancer, the Executioner had uncovered "something else." Beginning with vague whispers, fragmented rumors of a "joint in the desert," Bolan had gradually pieced together an admittedly incomplete portrait of something special brewing on the Tucson Mafia scene—"something else" worth further in-depth investigation.

Bolan had found the "joint in the desert" late on his sixth day in Tucson. He had come without preconceptions, expecting nothing and open to any opportunity for a "handle" on this latest phase of his unending war. What he found was an enigma. A solution without a mystery, an answer lacking the question. And so he had returned in darkness, seeking that question which would, in turn, lead him on to yet other questions and their ultimate solutions.

The Tucson Mafia's "joint in the desert" was a military-style compound covering some thirty acres and ringed with tall chain-link and barbed-wire fences. In daylight, long, squat buildings were visible near the heart of the compound, all darkened now in the predawn hours.

The big project of the Arizona Mafia was currently narcotics, the wholesale importation of marijuana and "brown" heroin by jeep, truck, and private plane across the 360-mile border shared by Arizona and Mexico. Of late, Federal narcotics officers had come to speak of an Arizona Corridor for drugs which threatened to equal and eventually eclipse the volume of the old French Connection routes from Europe. Dope and a readily accessible border had built the southwestern Mafia, but this apparent hardsite in the arid wastes carried little of the narcotics smell about it.

Sure, there was the paved airstrip running north to south along the western rim of the compound, and Bolan would not be shocked to learn that more than one plane load of Mexican drugs had found their touchdown point there. But the joint itself was clearly more than an isolated heroin depot, and Bolan knew it at a glance. The mob preferred isolated and inconspicuous sites for such landings, and the Tucson *mafiosi* would never have considered erecting fences and buildings to advertise their purpose.

The place was, theoretically, an outpost of the State Land Reclamation Commission, as proclaimed by the metal NO TRESPASSING signs on the perimeter. The official facade meant nothing to Bolan, and fifteen minutes of circuit riding in the guise of an idle rockhound had been enough to convince him that the cover was fraudulent. No canals or irrigation pipes crossed that perimeter, and the buildings, which he scanned casually through field glasses, lacked the nebulous "official" quality he had come to expect in sites devoted to scientific research at state expense.

No, the place was a hardsite—or had been at one time. Neither Bolan's daylight recon nor his silent nocturnal vigil had turned up more than a handful of hardmen moving too casually about their business. There was no open display of gunleather, but those guys inside the compound were hardmen all the same. Bolan read their pedigree from a distance as easily as if they had been uni-

7

formed. City boys, unfamiliar and uncomfortable with desert living, even in the mild heat of early spring. They dressed casually in blue jeans and fatigues, but they moved like men more accustomed to flashy, expensive suits and alligator shoes.

The Executioner meant to know their number and their purpose. He had opted for a soft probe, if at all possible, and had outfitted himself accordingly. He was in blacksuit and blackface. His "head weapon," the big silver .44 Automag, rode military web at his right hip. The silenced 9mm Beretta Brigadier, the "Belle," nestled in side-leather beneath his left armpit. Extra clips for both pistols circled his waist. Slit pockets in the legs of his skinsuit held a stiletto and other useful accessories. Black sneakers on his feet completed the doomsday ensemble.

Bolan had planned the infiltration for dawn, when the forces of heredity and chemistry override training to produce sluggishness and torpor in the most alert of sentries. That hour was fast approaching. Off to the east, across the dry bed of the Santa Cruz River, the first gray fingers of dawn backlighted the darker mass of Tucson. To the south and west, the San Xavier Indian Reservation lay in pitch blackness, its inhabitants awaiting nature's signal to open another day of struggle and deprivation. Bolan was on the south perimeter of the rectangular compound, where the wire barrier drew closest to the clump of buildings.

He had earlier tested the fence for electricity and found none. He removed a pair of wire cutters from their holster at his waist and cut an entrance through the chain-link barricade in five minutes of concentrated effort. And then he was inside, a deep blotch of shadow which had shifted from one side of the fence to the other as if following a moonbeam.

Inside the compound, Bolan moved with speed and purpose. He crossed the expanse of ground between fence and buildings in a semi-crouch, sacrificing some concealment for the greater speed of long strides. His target was the longest of the structures, a squat rectangle of corrugated steel which stood like the head of a "T" in relation to the other buildings. Bolan gained the midnight shadow of that wall without encountering obstacles and merged silently into it. A long moment passed as his straining ears and keen night vision scoured the blackness in search of foes he never found.

Satisfied that he was alone to this point, Bolan moved out, edging along the wall of the building. He had traversed one-third of the structure's length when he encountered a door, secured by an outside hasp and padlock. He crouched with his ear close to the door panel before touching the lock, striving in vain to pick up the telltale sounds of human presence. There were none. The lock yielded to the probings of a specially constructed pick, and the hasp swung open with a faint grating sound. Again Bolan froze, every muscle tense in anticipation of impending attack.

He gave the moment all the numbers, then slipped quickly inside to stygian darkness, electing to risk the advantage of a needle beam from his penlight. Folding chairs, small tables, metal lockers lining one wall—then yawning emptiness to the far wall where heavy mattresses formed a backdrop from ceiling to floor—just hanging there, suspended . . . and shot all to hell. Those mattresses were riddled with holes, their cotton innards trailing in spidery strands to the packed-earth floor. To Bolan's eyes it was obvious that the pads had formed a backdrop for an indoor shooting gallery, from which the actual targets had since been removed.

Interesting, sure, but not particularly revealing. More interesting was a small blackboard affixed to one wall behind the tables. Someone had been illustrating a talk—or a strategy of some type—with chalked arrows and other cryptic marks which, standing alone, had no meaning whatever. Beside the blackboard was posted a well marked-up street map of the city of Phoenix. Bolan removed the map and consigned it to a slit pocket as he moved silently outside.

The remainder of the compound was laid out before Bolan like a miniature town. Or, more precisely, like a miniature combat training base. A second glance revealed that the double row of "buildings" was in fact a mockup of a town, false fronts complete with occasional open doorways and windows. A make-believe town. Mack Bolan had seen this sort of town before.

It was a shooting gallery, or—more correctly—a combat range. The mockup was used by the military, the FBI, and many metropolitan police forces to hone the combat reflexes of their line personnel. The trainee walks through the "town," and life-size photos of friends, foes, and innocent bystanders pop into view in the vacant windows and doors. It was a hypothetical survival course, with the trainee required to make split-second decisions of life and death, whether to fire or hesitate, whether to live or die. Bolan himself had run a similar practice course on several occasions, earning a "master" rating each time.

Easing the silent Beretta from its sheath, the Executioner moved cautiously down that dark and lifeless street. As he walked, he was reminded of the climactic showdown in *High Noon*. The tall silent stranger with a gun, stalking his villainous prey as he fought to "clean up the town." Bolan did not overlook the apt comparison between that mythical crusade and his own grim war without end.

He paced off the street of that hollow town with measured strides, every sense on the alert for danger, the slim Beretta nosing out ahead of him like a sensor of peril. Bolan was ready, therefore, when a subtle alteration of the shadows to his left brought him spinning into a confrontation with death.

A dark man-shape filled one of those empty doorways, and faint starlight gleamed on polished gunmetal as the man brought his heavy automatic to bear on Bolan. The Beretta got there first, sneezing out a pair of silent words to discourage the foe. The deadly parabellum slugs sighed in on target, punching twin paths through head bone barely a finger's width apart. The human silhouette dematerialized, leaving the doorway empty again.

Bolan crossed quickly to the plywood facade, examining his fallen enemy as much by touch as by sight. A middle-aged man, his body lean and hard under the rough work clothes he had worn in life, the remaining features of his face thick and swarthy.

Mafia.

The Executioner moved on, stepping more quickly along the blackened street of the combat range. At the far end of the mock town he found deserted barracks and an equally empty combination kitchen-dining room. There was nothing exceptional about either building, nothing of interest to Mack Bolan.

The dead man had been alone.

Bolan knew it with certainty as he left that place behind, moving across the compound with no effort at concealment. The guy had been on nightwatch, in the wrong place at the wrong time. His tab had come due to the universe for past wrongs, and the bill had been collected in full. That was the end of it.

But not for Bolan.

He had come in search of a clue to the purpose of that enigmatic "joint in the desert." And, at least in part, he had that answer. The place was—*had been*—a school. A school of death, a finishing academy for gunmen.

And the pupils were gone.

The maneuvers Bolan had witnessed earlier had plainly been the mechanical actions of a cleanup crew, tidying in the wake of the Mafia's graduating class.

And where were those "graduates" now?

Already bent upon their missions of pain and death?

The mob had never taken this sort of trouble before to train its palace guard, and Bolan had no reason to believe they were starting now. The pupils of this death academy would be intended for some special postgraduation exercise.

The Executioner's Arizona blitz had begun as a relatively simple thrust against the heroin traffic, a logical culmination of Bolan's progress from the Cleveland hellgrounds, but it had suddenly become much more.

A new element had been introduced into the Arizona game—a wild card element that had to be identified and understood if the chains binding this desert state were to be broken. All the indicators pointed to the existence of a paramilitary force under mob sponsorship. Who were they? Where were they now? What was their mission? Such were the questions being raised by the answers discovered on this desert encampment.

A subliminal tremor shivered Bolan's spine.

What was awaiting the Executioner in these new hellgrounds?

He quit that place and returned quickly to the gully where he had stowed the warwagon. The answers would find him. He was positive of that. *Those* answers always seemed to find their way to Mack Bolan's door.

CHAPTER 2

JOKERS

The Mafia had come to Tucson in the 1940s, when enemies from without engaged the nation in global war, leaving the enemies within to devour the vitals of society. Niccolo "Nick" Bonelli, an underboss and junior partner of Cleveland's Bad Tony Morello, had visited the desert spa while recovering from gunshot wounds and decided to stay. Morello had looked askance at his new desert outpost, until Bonelli enlightened him about the miracles of geography and Mexican politics. Overnight Bad Tony's scorn had been converted to admiration for Bonelli's foresight. For three decades Nick Bonelli had mined the illicit Arizona goldfields in his master's behalf, always reserving a healthy slice of power and profit for himself. Of late, Bad Tony had become more concerned with his own eastern machinations, content to let Bonelli run his arid fiefdom at will, so

14

long as the usual percentage found its way home to the Cleveland coffers. And when at last Tony lost it all in his clash with Mack the Bastard Bolan, Nick Bonelli was on his own, free at last from the puppet master on Lake Erie.

Niccolo Bonelli, at age 55, now headed the most powerful Mafia family between the Rockies and the Pacific. He had climbed the ladder of illicit power from gambling, prostitution, and wartime black-marketeering to achieve ultimate status as the heroin king of the Southwest. His hopes and fortune lay south of the border, and the Mexican heroin his pilots ferried across from Sonora biweekly had financed Bonelli's excursion into more legitimate forms of enterprise. The California families relied heavily upon Nick's southern connection, as did the dons in Cleveland and Detroit. Augie Marinello had used Nick's services before he bought the farm in Pittsfield. Lately, rumor had it that the flow of drugs reached as far as Alaska and the boom towns opening along that last frontier.

Nick Bonelli's strong right arm, underboss, and heir apparent was his son Paul. Paul Bonelli had "legs," everybody said so. Legs and balls. He had "made his bones" with a contract hit at age nineteen and ably assisted in the family's administrative business ever since.

Bolan dredged these facts from his mental index file as he piloted the GMC warwagon north along Interstate Highway 19 into South Tucson. He caught the interchange onto Interstate 10 there, nosing the sleek battle cruiser across the desert toward Phoenix.

During his week in Tucson, the Executioner had searched out Nick Bonelli's hardsite home

15

and his major centers of operation. Automated intelligence "Collectors" were installed on the phone terminals of the hardsite, Paul Bonelli's suburban palace, and the desert *capo's* major underground clearinghouse. The warwagon's super-sophisticated electronic collection gear could reap the harvest of that data in a ten-second drive-by, and Bolan felt secure in leaving Tucson behind him for the moment.

All of Bolan's combat senses told him that the immediate crisis lay to the north in Phoenix. His days of reconnaissance had uncovered no likely hiding place in Tucson for a paramilitary troop such as the one he sought, and the captured map of Phoenix was another pointer to the next battlefield.

But Bolan had no idea what he would find there.

Phoenix is the state capital and the seat of Maricopa County, widely proclaimed as one of the nation's fastest-growing cities. Bolan's preblitz recon had found tourism, mining, and the manufacture of chemicals and electronics gear vying for first place as the state's leading industry there—plentiful targets for a Mafia strike force, but Bolan could not read the minds of unknown men at long range.

Phoenix was also the *mob* capital of Arizona, the seat of government for a corrupt ruling commission with fingers in every important pie in the state. And these guys were not Mafia, at least not in the blood. Second and third generation descendants of immigrants from Eastern Europe, amoral renegades paying blasphemous lip service to the religion of their fathers. Jews in name, yes, but Nazis in their souls, savages and cannibals devoted to the subversion of every ideal held sacred by their ancestors. They blackened the name of their religion just as the Mafia godfathers blackened the name of an entire race.

Yes, Bolan knew them. And he knew their city. His computer banks and mental mug file were crammed with their names and various connections to the workings of the Mafia's ruling *commissione*. Wherever the Mafia had grown and prospered since Prohibition, these other savages were there as well, ever clinging to the shadows as the more flamboyant *amici* filled headlines and mortuaries, lending their advice and financial acumen where it was lacking in their Mafia comrades. Siegel, Buchalter, Cohen, Lansky. Bolan knew their names and their games.

And he had wanted no part of them in Arizona.

Sure, they were well deserving of the Executioner's attention. He had hung the mark of the beast on one of them as recently as the Cleveland battle.

But Mack Bolan needed no new enemies. He had more than he could handle in a lifetime simply dealing with the Mafia's brothers of the blood, where the battle lines were more or less clearly drawn, the enemies generally recognizable at a glance.

Any expansion of the war would necessarily mean an escalation of uncertainty and the corresponding potential for disastrous mistakes. The fine line between innocent bystanders and civilian savages would necessarily become more difficult to distinguish.

In the past, Bolan had deliberately avoided confrontation with what one observer of the syndicate scene had dubbed the "Kosher Nostra," but there could be no avoiding them now.

He was headed full tilt into their capital city.

And the whole deck was wild now in the Arizona game.

The Executioner was in effect facing not one, but *two* crime syndicates, and he had no idea at the moment whether they were cooperating or at war. And to complicate matters further, there was that lethal "something else," Nick Bonelli's own private army, a paramilitary force of unknown size and strength, traveling unknown paths toward completion of an unknown mission.

Too many wild cards for the Executioner to formulate campaign strategy in advance. He would have to play by ear in Arizona, riding his instincts to the ultimate end of success or total destruction.

Bolan punched in a geo-plot on the warwagon's console viewing screen, consulting the automated index for the microframe desired, then locking in the display for the area he was traveling.

Interstate 10 approaches Phoenix from due south, looping through the suburb of Tempe before curving away northwest past Sky Harbor International Airport and into the downtown heart of Arizona's capital as Interstate 17. Bolan flipped on the overhead light to consult the "liberated" street map of Phoenix which was covered with cryptic markings. There were thick black crosses, which he took to designate some sort of staging areas, and four separate potential targets had been circled with bold strokes. Drawn between the staging areas and target zones were the routes of access and retreat, with primary routes marked in red and emergency alternates in green.

Bolan recognized three of the targets—one from simple knowledge of geography and the other two from a working acquaintance with the Phoenix crime scene. The fourth target remained an enigma, but for the moment three were enough.

Two of the targets were private homes, and Bolan recognized them by the street names and progressive block numbers printed on the map as belonging to the major organized crime figures of the city. If an inter-mob war *was* brewing, these targets would come as no surprise.

The third target riveted Bolan's attention.

The state capitol building.

Bolan urged his warwagon on to greater speed, giving the big Toronado engine its head in the race toward Phoenix and an almost certain confrontation with holocaust.

In fact, only the death card was certain now in what had started as the Tucson game, then shifted to the Phoenix game.

It was the *Arizona* game now.

The other cards were all jokers, and the jokers were wild.

CHAPTER 3

PARADISE

Bolan swung the warwagon off the Interstate and onto Central Avenue, powering smoothly along the thoroughfare toward the heart of Phoenix. He passed Union Station and the county office complex on his left, and soon spied the multimillion dollar bulk of the new Civic Plaza looming two blocks over to his right on the east flank.

The Executioner's target of the moment was not downtown. Technically, it was not in Phoenix at all. He was homing on the elite suburb of Paradise Valley and had elected the Central route to save time wasted on a maze of residential streets. The sleek battle cruiser powered on, leaving behind the campus of Maricopa Tech and the Phoenix Art Center in its wake. Bolan left Central far from the heart of town, swinging east onto Camelback Road and homing on his target as common homes began to bloom and blossom into mansions.

Bolan was well versed on the peculiar pedigree of Paradise Valley. The exclusive "in" community boasted three private country clubs, yet another private golf course, and a theoretically public "tennis ranch," and some years back the socialite inhabitants had cast their mayoral votes for gambler and stock swindler Gus Greenbaum. Old Gus hadn't been a *bad* mayor really, since he spent most of his time visiting with co-investors in Las Vegas gaming ventures. The Nevada connections had proven hazardous for Gus, and he went the way of all flesh in 1958, when one of those dissatisfied partners slit his throat from ear to ear and left him leaking on the posh carpet of his palatial home in Paradise.

And Paradise had been truly a paradise for the Phoenix mob, a retreat and sanctuary, a home away from the daily details of corruption and murder, a breath of clean air amid the reek of the syndicate charnel house.

Mack Bolan came to Paradise one morning in early spring and found the Serpent already there ... or, at least, the Serpent's lair.

He drove on by and pulled up three blocks further on, beside the rolling greenery of a well-trimmed public park. Selecting a nondescript jumpsuit and blue hardhat from his wardrobe of disguises, the Executioner quickly transformed himself into a telephone lineman. A tool box, safety belts, and climbing spikes completed the outfit.

Bolan quit the warwagon, jangling off along the quiet lane toward his destination. He chose a phone pole at one corner of the walled estate he sought and began to climb with easy practiced movements. His crow's nest at the terminal box provided him with an excellent vantage point for viewing the entire estate: scattered trees, gently rolling grounds, and a charmingly extravagant manor house at the end of the graveled drive.

A dragon lived within those walls, a corrupt old serpent in human form. Morris Kaufman—Moe to his old friends in Detroit and the new ones here in Paradise—had once been jokingly referred to as "the Yiddish Augie Marinello," a reference to the Mafia's late and unlamented Boss of Bosses. A joke, of course, but there was more truth than humor in the analogy, and the joke was on Phoenix society.

Like Nick Bonelli, Moe Kaufman had come west in adversity, one propitious jump ahead of a crusading grand jury in Detroit. And he had built an empire in the desert, growing along with his adopted city in wealth and influence. He outranked Bonelli in seniority and sheer wealth. More importantly, he pulled the political strings for much of the Grand Canyon State from his *de facto* position as the mentor and financier of rising lights in government. Of late there had been speculation as to how far his influence might reach into the upper ranks of state government and beyond, but one investigative reporter had already "committed suicide" in recent months, and the rest was silence.

A dragon, yeah. A scabrous old parasite living to eat the bowels of the society that sheltered him. But maybe a dragon in trouble.

The Kaufman estate was one of those "marks" on Bolan's captured battle map.

Bolan opened the terminal box and plugged in. He found a line in use on the second try, and what he heard instantly riveted his full attention. A man's hard voice was growling in the earpiece.

". . . else is here. She's alone here with the houseman and a maid."

"Shit!" An answering male voice, deep, with a hint of southern twang.

"We had to burn the houseman. So now what?"

"Dammit! *He* was supposed to be there!"

"Think we should wait?"

"No! No waiting! Did the maid get a look at you?"

"Sure she got a look."

"Okay. Take care of that. And put a sack on Miss Boobs and drag her over here. We'll bring the guy to us."

"Ten-four, gotcha. We're on our way."

The line went dead.

Bolan hurriedly clipped in a miniature recorder-transceiver and tidied the tap with some quick camouflage, then quit that perch, descending immediately and shedding his lineman's tools as he trotted toward the ironwork entrance to the Kaufman estate.

A car engine coughed to life somewhere within those grounds, and the squeal of tires along the drive signaled the coming confrontation. Bolan opened the jumpsuit and sprung the silent Beretta from its armpit sheath as he jogged into that meet. The iron gate was humming and rattling as it slowly withdrew along the remote-controlled pulley chain. A four-door sedan was approaching, slowing for the gate. In the split second before his brain impulses were translated into lethal action, Bolan ran a rapid sizing on that fated vehicle.

Four heads were behind that glass—two guys in front, another guy and a young woman in the rear. With hardly a break in stride, Bolan swung into the confrontation with Beretta raised and steadied in classic combat crouch. The silenced weapon coughed four times in rapid succession, dispatching two parabellum manglers into the auto grillwork and two more at precise points through the windshield. Two heads snapped back, imparting a mingled spray of life forces into the compact atmosphere, splattering the other passengers with wet streamers of crimson and gray.

The sedan lurched to a stop, its punctured radiator spluttering its death rattle. The girl was going crazy, her mouth yawning in a soundless scream, but her companion in the rear seat retained more self-composure. A side door sprang open and ejected that hardman in a diving headlong roll, his frantic hands clawing for gunleather. The Beretta chugged out a deadly double message, and the guy's graceful dive suddenly became an awkward blood-drenched wallow of death.

Bolan moved swiftly to the car and leaned inside. The front seaters were both dead as hell, the backs of their skulls missing and replaced by sodden muck. The fourth passenger, however, was very much alive.

And, quite naturally, scared as hell.

Her screams were winding down to a breathless series of panting little gasps. At sight of Bolan and that ominous black blaster, she began screaming again, shrill, strangled sounds, eyes bulging and face reddening. She was dressed only in a wraparound bathrobe, and that was blotched with spreading patches of blood.

24

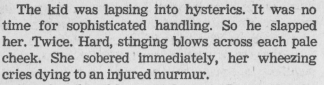

The kid was lapsing into hysterics. It was no time for sophisticated handling. So he slapped her. Twice. Hard, stinging blows across each pale cheek. She sobered immediately, her wheezing cries dying to an injured murmur.

"You're okay," he said, the tone firm and reassuring. "Cool it. Who are you?"

The girl's mouth worked for a couple of seconds before the sounds emerged. "I—I'm Sharon Kaufman."

Oh yeah. Wonderful. Bolan's cup fairly runneth over. He pulled the girl out, slung her across his shoulder, and without wasting a precious moment, hurried to the warwagon with his "prize."

The going was not all that easy, though. She was no frail wisp of a girl but a substantial chunk of womanhood with long, flowing lines and plenty of nice womanflesh packed onto that feminine frame. Bolan sized her out at about 130 to 140 pounds and close to six feet in height. If she'd wanted to put up a fight, he would have had his hands full. But there was no fight in this one. She was still obviously terrified, confused, perhaps only partially conscious.

He deposited her on a bunk in the warwagon and peeled away the bloodied robe. She shrank from that invasion of personal privacy but made no move to interfere with the inspection. "Miss Boobs," for sure. Not just big but big and firm, proud and—in most any other circumstances—tantalizing.

"Please!" she whispered. "Don't . . . don't . . . ."

"Relax," he said pleasantly. "I'm just looking for hurts." He closed the robe and told her, "You pass. A-OK. None of the blood is yours. You'll feel a lot better after you've scrubbed it off." He pointed out the shower stall to her. "Don't waste the water. It's a small tank."

He patted her hand and gave her a friendly smile, then went forward to send the battle cruiser to softer ground. Circling the streets of Paradise, Bolan drove with one portion of his mind while using the rest to probe the new dimensions of his problem.

Moe Kaufman had been the hit team's primary target, no doubt about it. *He* wasn't home, the voice on the phone had said—the girl would bring *him* to "us." So far it played. But had the crew been looking to hit the Jewish *capo* or merely abduct him? And to what ultimate end?

Sharon Kaufman was yet another wild card in the game. The Serpent's daughter, a pearl before swine. With the old man missing, her abduction had been the logical and inevitable move. If the mountain won't come to Mohammed ...

And where did Bolan's new "prize" fall in the scheme of things? A healthy and apparently vibrant young woman, but a serpent's daughter all the same. Where would she stand when the cut came?

Another imponderable in the Arizona game.

The players were multiplying like rabbits, and it was getting hard to tell them apart without a program. There was more than one serpent in Paradise now, and they were at war.

Bolan found himself joining the Arizona game late, already several moves behind. But he had captured a queen on his opening gambit, and it just might be enough. Enough to scatter the players, and maybe—just maybe—enough to upset the whole damn board.

The Executioner drove on deeper into Paradise.

Searching for serpents.

CHAPTER 4

PROS

Jim Hinshaw was unhappy, and rightly so. A consummate professional, accustomed to excellence in every undertaking, he naturally possessed a low tolerance for failure. It rankled, offending his sense of order, upsetting the sensation of control that he relished in every situation. He had invested six months of his time and over ten grand of Nick Bonelli's money to insure his control on the current project, only to find his first thrust blunted and broken by unknown forces.

The Kaufman snatch should have gone off without a hitch. Hinshaw's spotters had staked the old man out for an honest-to-God solid month, charting his every move day and night, and he'd never once left the house before nine in the morning.

Until today. *The* day.

Hinshaw had abandoned his belief in miracles

at age six, when his father stepped out for a quick beer and never came home, so Kaufman's absence had to be ascribed to either freakish coincidence or advance warning. Ever the realist, he opted for advance warning.

And that meant a traitor.

Not within Hinshaw's troops, he was reasonably sure of that. His men were loyal. Loyal to the project out of greed and, at another level, loyal to *him* out of mingled fear and respect.

Hinshaw admired loyalty in his equals and demanded it from his subordinates. It was one of the qualities that marked the line between amateurs and pros, between a mob and a skilled team of operatives. It was essential to the maintenance of order.

Order demanded that Hinshaw salvage the situation in Phoenix. *Loyalty* and skilled professionalism would make that salvation possible.

Hinshaw began checking off the pluses and minuses of the current situation. Minuses first: Kaufman had slipped through their fingers, the broad—Kaufman's daughter—had managed to get away, too, and three of his men were stretched out in a refrigerated drawer downtown. That was 10 percent of his force out of action in the first skirmish, a skirmish that should not have occurred in the first place.

On the plus side, their cop downtown seemed convinced that one man alone had pulled the morning hit. Hinshaw was inclined to think his team had overlooked one of Kaufman's housemen, allowing the guy to take them by surprise on the way out. Carelessness kills. Awaiting Hinshaw's next order were the other pluses: Angel Morales and Floyd Worthy, Hinshaw's oldest friends from

'Nam, his personal "secret weapons." And backing them up, twenty-five of the meanest, ass-kickingest boys who ever pulled a rod in Tucson, *his* boys now, courtesy of Nick Bonelli.

Hinshaw owed a lot to Bonelli, for all the trust and power and money—yeah, that counted, too—that the Tucson *capo* had supplied over the months. Nick Bonelli's goals and hopes were *his* goals now, *his* hopes, and by God, he couldn't bring himself to tell the old man that somebody had screwed up on phase one. He could still pull it out, and he damn well *would*. He owed that to Mr. Bonelli. And to himself.

Hinshaw punched buttons on the desk intercom and growled a summons. The office door opened to admit two men. They nodded greetings and moved toward empty chairs. They lacked ramrod spines and the overall military carriage that marked Hinshaw, yet they moved with an identical grace and power, emitting lethal vibrations into the room.

Pros, yeah. *Men*.

Angel Morales. Small and lean, straight black hair framing finely chiseled Latin features, sensual lips curving slightly in a little smile which widened to a grin in the heat of combat. And Floyd Worthy. Tall, grim, black as the ace of spades, his restless hands ever moving, at peace only when holding one of the weapons that he loved.

Hinshaw felt better already, stronger, more confident. They were a team all right, and together, Hinshaw knew, they could move mountains.

Worthy opened the dialogue with his deep, drawling voice. "What's the word, my man?"

"The word is that our boys were iced by *one*

man. I take that to mean that Kaufman has no troops in the field—*yet.* If we move quick enough, we should be able to cut our losses and salvage the play."

"Target Baker?" The question came from Morales.

"Affirmative. We still need a hostage for our hole card. Floyd, I want you to take personal charge of this action, and be sure the boys understand that we need the pigeon alive. Cold meat won't get us the time of day."

Worthy gave him an unemotional "Roger," the big ebony hands opening and clenching in slow rhythm.

"Take a half-dozen men with you," Hinshaw continued. "The last team came up short." There was no trace of regret in his voice as he dismissed the deaths, merely a recognition of tactical error.

"I can handle it," Worthy assured him, risking a narrow smile for the first time.

"I have every confidence," Hinshaw told his friend, returning the grim smile. "Angel, you're on backup and communications. Commit minimal reinforcements as a last resort. Emphasize that *last.*"

"Gotcha," Morales replied. "Floyd don't need any help on a run like this, do ya Floyd?"

"Made in the shade," Worthy rumbled in response.

"Right. That's all." Hinshaw dropped his eyes to a folder of papers on the desk, and the other men recognized the dismissal for what it was, letting themselves out.

Jim Hinshaw was no longer upset. He felt good now, powerful, worthy of Nick Bonelli's confidence. It would be the old squeeze play, just like

31

in 'Nam, bring the enemy to his knees and keep him there. The old Special Forces motto came back to him: *When you've got 'em by the balls, their hearts and minds will follow.* Yeah, and their fortunes, too, any damn thing you demand. But first the squeeze, the all-important stranglehold.

Yeah, *balls* was the name of the game.

The GMC motor home which served as Bolan's warwagon was parked on a wooded lane in Echo Canyon Park. Bolan and Sharon Kaufman sat on opposite ends of the same fold-down bunk, he still in blacksuit and she looking almost childlike in the voluminous folds of his robe. Almost childlike, but not quite. Even in that outsize garment, she was a hell of a lot of woman, and no clothing could disguise the fact.

Bolan reluctantly pulled his eyes away from there and caught hers over the lip of an upraised coffee mug. He found lingering fear in that gaze, but she offered him a tentative smile as she lowered the mug and haltingly told him, "I—I don't know what to say . . . except . . . thanks . . . I—I guess."

His eyes remained warm, but the voice was ice-tinged as he replied, "You could say a lot more than that."

Her gaze fell to the coffee cup. She said nothing.

"Your father is Moe Kaufman."

"Of course."

"He's in trouble."

"Yes I . . . I gathered as much. What did those men want?"

"They wanted his head. Someone still does.

That's why they tried to snatch you. Your head was a means to his. It's the big game, Miss Kaufman. Why did you think they took you?"

"I—it didn't—I didn't have time to think about it. Everything happened so fast. Who *are* you?"

"I'm the guy who snatched you back. But you are in your own hands now. Walk away, if that's what you want. Return home. But I advise that you don't."

Fear was becoming a living presence between them. Her eyes receded, shrinking from his gaze as her mind obviously tumbled with a thousand questions and perhaps ten times as many logical answers. "What should I do then?" she asked.

He spread his hands as he suggested, "Talk to me."

She hesitated. "About what?"

"You could start with your father's business associates."

"What? I don't—"

"Nick Bonelli." It was neither a statement nor a question, it was simply there, hanging between them in the sudden silence.

"Well . . . yes, Mr. Bonelli and my father are friends. I believe they're partners in some sort of business venture in Tucson."

"The partnership is dissolving," Bolan told her grimly.

"What?" More tension in the young voice now, edging out the confusion.

"The men who grabbed you were Bonelli's."

"What? How do you . . . *who are you?*"

"The name's Bolan."

There was no immediate comprehension on that young face, merely deepening puzzlement.

"Should I . . . haven't I heard your name somewhere?"

"Could be. Your father and his ex-partner are quite familiar with it."

"How do you know my father?"

"By reputation mostly. Until this morning I was his worst enemy."

"Bolan? *Bolan*!" She was still chewing that one over when she suddenly made the connection, and her pretty face lost another shade of color. "Oh my God! Are you *that* Bolan?"

"Last of the line," he told her without humor.

"But . . . you're supposed to . . . I mean . . . you fight the Mafia."

Bolan said nothing, letting the impact of her own realization sink in.

"Oh no, you can't think that my father is involved with the Mafia?"

"Bonelli—your father's business partner—is the *capo* of Tucson," he told her.

She seemed stunned. "C—capo?"

"*Capo mafioso*. The local godfather. The mould on top of the cheese. Your father has been in bed with the guy for years."

"I've heard some of those stories," she responded, some of the flush returning to her cheeks in a wave of defensive reaction to Bolan's words. "I don't believe them. But suppose Mr. Bonelli is . . . what you say. My father is a businessman. He needs . . . contacts."

"You met some of those contacts this morning."

"But why would Mr. Bonelli want to harm my father?"

"That's the big question. I'm in Phoenix for the

answer. One thing I *do* know. Those guys were pros, and they didn't come to town alone. Their back-up crews will be looking for your father now, if they haven't already found him."

"They won't have. If my father doesn't want to be found . . . well, he just isn't, that's all." Her head and shoulders slumped ever so slightly as she spoke, and Bolan knew with certainty that Sharon Kaufman had indeed heard "some of those stories" about her father. And wondered, no doubt, about certain odd circumstances and behavior at various times, about the swarthy visitors and the gravel-voiced nocturnal phone calls.

Yeah, Sharon Kaufman knew or guessed—or, more likely, feared to know—the truth about her "businessman" father.

She broke the silence after a long and thoughtful pause. "Did you mean what you said? About my being free to leave?"

"Any time you choose. I don't draft civilians."

"But you *would* like my help, wouldn't you?"

"I don't have anything to trade, Sharon."

"My father's life?" she suggested hopefully.

"I won't make promises I can't keep," he told her coldly. Then he added, with more compassion, "For what it's worth, I didn't come to Phoenix to hit your father. I could probably achieve that simply by leaving town and giving his 'friends' a free hand. My goal, so far as possible, is to avert a street war and prevent any mob faction from seizing total control. I'll pursue those goals by any means necessary. Fair warning."

Sharon Kaufman thought about that for several long moments before raising her eyes again to meet Bolan's gaze. "All right," she said

35

simply. "I'll help you, to a point. But I won't endanger my father!"

"Fine. We understand each other," he told her. But he knew very well that they did not.

CHAPTER 5

UNDERSTANDINGS

Sharon Kaufman gathered her breath, mentally gauging what she could afford to tell the big man in black. She was more than a little frightened by his words and grim demeanor, and still shaken by the morning's grisly events, but she sensed traces of warmth in his voice, more than a touch of heart behind those graveyard eyes. At length she began to speak slowly, haltingly, weighing her words carefully to present them in the desired context.

"About an hour before those men arrived, my father got a phone call from Ike Ruby."

"I know Ruby," Bolan told her. "Go on."

Sharon was startled, suddenly off balance, no longer certain how much the big man already knew. She fought to collect her thoughts again before continuing.

"The call seemed important. My father acted ... well, not angry, exactly ... upset."

Bolan broke into her musing train of thought. "So he went over to see Ruby."

"I—I don't know. Honestly. He may have, but ... he only told me that he had to go out for a while." She hesitated, then added, "My father and Ike are in business together. They might have met at Daddy's office ... if at all. I just don't know where he went."

The ice returned to the big man's voice as he responded to that. "Okay. Where can I drop you?"

It startled her. She was not prepared for such quick dismissal. "I—but—what ...?"

"I believe you. We're square. Let's end it on that note."

"It isn't ended, though, is it?" she ventured meekly, adding, "For my father."

"I'm afraid not," he replied gently.

She read that loud and clear. Lifelong protests rose automatically through the tightening throat. "You have it all wrong. My father is a decent man. He has *business* enemies ... *political* enemies ... but this other is ... well, it's just not true!"

"Where do I drop you?" he asked again, ignoring the impassioned protest.

"Ike Ruby has been a second father to me! I've called him 'Uncle Ike' as long as I can remember." She thought she saw a flicker of human light in those steely eyes and leapt quickly to summon it again. "Please. I sense a—a fairness in you. Why save me only to—to cast me back into the flames!"

He sighed wearily as he told her, "I'm casting

you nowhere. All I want from Kaufman and Ruby is the truth. I can't very well get that if I can't find them, can I?"

She made a quick decision, quivering lungs fairly bursting with it. "Then I'll just go along and help you find it."

He showed her a genuine if tiny smile as he replied, "No way."

"Why not? I have a stake in this, too. I have a right."

The smile departed as he grimly responded to that. "The right to die?" Those incredible eyes flashed with some inner misery. "We all have that right. But I don't have to help you exercise it."

There was a recognizable finality in that response. Her gaze dropped to her lap and she fidgeted. Then, in a barely audible whisper, she said, "I can't go back home."

"No," he quietly agreed.

"I—I'll need to make a telephone call."

He sighed and pointed out the instrument, instructed her on its use, and watched unemotionally as she made arrangements to "crash" with a college friend. From that point, conversation with the big, quiet man was confined entirely to small talk and directions to the drop point.

It was a brief ride, the destination being a "singles" apartment complex off North Central avenue, almost in the shadow of St. Joseph's Hospital. She used that time to visually probe the interior of the fantastic vehicle and to wonder pointedly about the grim secrets it carried. A vehicle of *war*, certainly, as grim and threatening as the silent man who piloted it so casually through the Phoenix streets. He pulled out beyond the complex to methodically circle the neighborhood, thoroughly "casing" and probing that quiet neighborhood before pulling to the curb on a deserted side street behind the complex.

She rose from the seat and prepared to leave him, turning in the doorway for one more attempt at reaching him. "Mr. Bolan . . . I . . . ."

"No promises, Sharon," he reminded her in a gentle voice.

She began to say more, thought better of it, and left him, saying simply, "Thank you again." She hurried across the damp lawn toward the apartments, pausing briefly at the entranceway to watch the motor home as it rounded a corner and disappeared.

Sharon Kaufman turned and hastened to her own destination, her young face set in lines of grim determination. She would make her own promises.

Bolan knew Ike Ruby, all right. The girl had called Ruby a businessman, but the Executioner knew him as the chief enforcer and general staff officer of Moe Kaufman's desert empire. A native of the Bronx, Ruby had been an early protege of Lepke Buchalter in the labor wars before migrating westward toward his ultimate destiny as Kaufman's strong right arm. His rap sheet included seven arrests for first-degree murder, with one indictment and no convictions. And that was only the tip of the iceberg, for despite the periodic disappearance of opposition partisans and persistent rumors of a graveyard in the desert, Ruby had been unhampered by investigation or arrest for the past quarter-century.

A "businessman," yeah. Read that "cannibal."

Mack Bolan knew Ike Ruby, all right, and

somebody else knew him, too. The little mobster's estate was another of those "marks" on the captured map of Phoenix. Like his master, Ike Ruby was a target, and Bolan realized that he might already be too late for his "talk" with the guy. Not that he was bleeding over the fate of a decadent savage, far from it. Other circumstances might find Ike Ruby on the Executioner's own hit parade. But right now Bolan needed a score card for the Phoenix game, and Kaufman's right arm might be the one to supply it.

Bolan urged the Toronado power plant to greater speed as he homed on the Ruby estate, his near-photographic memory displaying the map of Phoenix streets for navigation. His target lay to the north and west of Camelback Park, within an easy rifle shot of the Interstate highway. He found it easily and circled the walled grounds in a brief recon, senses alert for any traces of hostile presence.

He found those traces immediately. The front gates to the place were open wide, and mental alarm bells jangled at the flagrant breach of security. He could see nothing else beyond the protective walls except scattered treetops and a tiled roof about seventy-five yards back.

He parked the warwagon and quickly outfitted himself for action. Big Thunder, the .44 Automag, went at his right hip to supplement the silent Beretta. A light machine pistol went around his neck, and clips for the weapons filled his belt. He briefly contemplated a rack of small grenades, then decided against them and put the battlewagon behind him.

Bolan ignored the beckoning front gate, opting for an entrance over the north wall. The grounds rolled away before him, dotted with trees at irregular intervals. His attention immediately centered on the house, a long low structure in the Spanish style, its red tile roof supported by thick adobe walls. A long crew wagon was idling at the front door, with a dark man-shape at the wheel, another lounging too casually against the passenger's side. A tall guy, well dressed, black, stiffening suddenly as staccato reports of gunfire erupted within the house.

Those shots galvanized Bolan, and he took advantage of the outside man's preoccupation to make his sprint for the house. He hit the side door with a flying kick and plunged inside, his light chatter gun at the ready.

An empty room sneered at him. From beyond the doorway opposite, a second burst of fire exploded, the reports hollow and thunderous. He crossed to the door and slid it open a crack, scanning the hellgrounds beyond through that narrow aperture.

Two guys were barricaded inside the kitchen, directing revolver fire into the parlor from behind an overturned oaken table. Three guys were returning that fire from behind heavily padded furniture in the living room. A riddled corpse was sprawled in the no man's land between those guns, and neither side showed signs of budging. Bolan caught a fleeting glimpse of Ike Ruby's bald head as he popped up to peg a shot at the invaders.

Bolan announced his entry into the battle with a short burst from the chopper. The deadly stream hit one of the invaders broadside, ripping him open from armpit to hip and punching him sideways across an ornate coffee table. The firing spluttered to a halt as four pairs of eyes swung toward Bolan's position, each side evaluating the new arrival in terms of personal jeopardy and need. Ike Ruby recognized help and cackled in triumph, rising from a crouch with his pistol barking an assist for the new ally. The hardmen in the parlor recoiled and tracked about, weapons seeking a new target in their desperate race for life.

Bolan was faster, stitching the first guy across the chest with a zipper of steel-jacketed slugs and sweeping him aside. The last hardman broke cover, crouching, his shotgun swinging uncertainly between targets for a fatal half-second too long. A deadly crossfire of machine gun and revolver slugs spun him like a top, blood spurting from a dozen mortal wounds as he corkscrewed to the floor. A dying finger clenched reflexively and his shotgun boomed toward Ruby and the houseman.

Peripheral images crowded Bolan's vision. On the right, Ruby's houseman going over backward in a spray of crimson, clapping reddened hands to his exploding skull. To the left, a looming form blackening the doorway, sunlight gleaming dully on gunmetal.

It was the big black from outside, an M-16 clutched in businesslike fashion against his hip. Bolan and the black man poised in that confrontation for a moment frozen in eternity, faint recognition crackling between them like electric current. Then Bolan was backpedaling and plunging to the floor as flame spluttered from that deadly muzzle and a stream of 5.56 tumblers chewed up the doorway. Bullets raked the walls, showering Bolan with adobe chips and splinters of wood. For a long second he was pinned there, unmoving, as the leaden wand of death stroked the air above him. Then it tracked on, seeking other targets in the room beyond, thumping through heavy wood to rip a scream from human lips in there.

It ended as suddenly as it began, and Bolan was in instant motion, the chopper nosing ahead of him as he reentered the silent hellgrounds. Outside, through the open doorway, the rasp of spinning tires on gravel telegraphed the end of the engagement. Taillights were winking through the front gate even as Bolan gained the porch.

He let it go, returning to the slaughterhouse within.

Bodies were draped around the furniture, but Bolan ignored them as he went in search of Ike Ruby. He found him stretched out behind the shattered remains of the oaken dining table. Slugs had stitched him across the chest, and each pained breath brought blood welling up from mangled lungs to soak his torn pajama top.

The guy was dying hard. His vision was going in and out of focus as he squinted up at Bolan, words of warning rasping in his throat. Ruby obviously thought Bolan had been sent by Kaufman to help out, and he was determined to get his message out before it was too late.

"Tell . . . tell Moe . . . couldn't reach Weiss . . . couldn't tip him off . . . ." The guy's head was lolling crazily about, breath wheezing in his throat and burbling through the holes in his chest at the same time. "Tell Moe . . . ."

"I'll tell him," Bolan assured the corpse, and then he quit the place, quickly retracing his path to the warwagon.

Ruby's dying plea echoed in the Executioner's

mind as he fired the warwagon and left the neighborhood behind. *Tell Moe that I couldn't reach Weiss.* A fragmentary message, sure, the garbled last words of a delirious and dying man, but suddenly as clear as crystal to the Executioner.

Another piece of the Arizona jigsaw puzzle dropped jarringly into place. A picture was forming in Bolan's mind, a confused and admittedly incomplete picture, to be sure, but a chilling one all the same. The game was assuming unexpected proportions, and new players were coming out of the woodwork on every side—most recently a dark and deadly face which Bolan vaguely recognized but could not immediately identify.

Bolan drove on, his jaw set in grim determination, mind intent on the dying concern of Ike Ruby.

The Executioner had a message to deliver.

To a United States senator named Weiss.

CHAPTER 6

CONNECTIONS

Senator Abraham Weiss liked to describe himself in campaign speeches as a self-made man. It sounded good to the voters. Of course, there were always a few spiteful and politically motivated critics to dispute the claim. Weiss liked to describe those critics to the voting public as scavengers, with their stories of how he had inherited the family business from his late father, without investing either his own money or original creative ideas. That was nonsense. Hadn't it been Abe who, mere days after his father's funeral, had expanded into marketing and shipment, too, forging close ties with the local Teamster leadership? And wasn't it Abe who had used his business and political connections to place brother David on the Board of directors of Greater Southwestern Savings and Loan, thereby broadening the Weiss empire into real estate investment?

The same bleeding hearts and sob-sisters who blasted Abe Weiss for his business investments were constantly harping about his political connections. They were always pointing to his friendship with Moe Kaufman as if there was something wrong with one lifelong pal contributing to the other's campaign fund. They blamed Weiss for following Moe's suggestion that he run for County Supervisor back in '49 and blasted him for delivering a eulogy at old Gus Greenbaum's funeral in '58. But what the hell, hadn't Gus been a fellow servant of the people and former mayor of Weiss' own home town? The sniveling vultures especially loved to pick at Abe for accepting Kaufman's financial support in three successful Senate campaigns, making wild charges about corruption and conflict of interest.

Weiss publicly dismissed those charges with the contempt they deserved, always ready to explain his swelling bank account as the result of life insurance dividends, and the resultant patronage to Kaufman's handpicked men as mere coincidence. What could be more natural than for lifelong friends to see each other socially from time to time, whether at home in Phoenix or during an expense-paid visit to one of Moe's hotels in Vegas? What *really* upset his opponents, Weiss told reporters, was his longtime stand against creeping socialism and his staunch defense of innocent businessmen facing criminal harassment by agents of the Justice Department's task force on organized crime.

Mack Bolan was familiar with the accusations against Weiss, and with the senator's protestations of innocence. More importantly, Bolan was familiar with the facts behind the charges and

47

countercharges. Abraham Weiss was a "made man" from the word go, most lately the prime mover behind a Senate inquisition aimed at Hal Brognola and his fellow federal warriors against the Mafia. Bolan could discern the fine hand of puppet-master Moe Kaufman in those Star Chamber proceedings and in other Capitol Hill maneuvers which "coincidentally" served the interests of the Phoenix mob.

Ike Ruby's dying words had been merely the confirmation of a certainty, yet they added sinister new dimensions to the Arizona game. For if Moe Kaufman felt it necessary to "tip Weiss off" about impending events, there might be much more at stake in Phoenix than an old-style street war between ethnic antagonists.

Bolan was well aware that Weiss had been mentioned by the press of late as a long-shot "dark horse" contender in the next presidential race. A tenuous lead, sure, no more than a pipe dream perhaps, but still food for thought.

A "made man" in the White House?

Sure. Why not?

Between them, Kaufman and Weiss surely had the savvy and political connections to insure "favorite son" backing for the candidate. And beyond that? If Kaufman remained in good standing with the national organization, the full weight and influence of the Mafia and its minions might be thrown behind the white knight from Arizona.

But how *did* Kaufman stand with his former *amici* in the Mafia? Was the latest thrust by Nick Bonelli and company merely a local power play or much more?

Sinister implications, yeah, even without the full story.

Part of the answer lay with the captured battle map of Phoenix and the marks around the state capitol, where Weiss maintained an office. And it took the Executioner less than five minutes with a Phoenix phone directory to confirm the residence of Abraham Weiss as target number four on Bonelli's campaign chart.

Abe Weiss was part of the Phoenix game plan whether or not he'd become aware of it. So was another whose dark face nagged at Bolan's photographic memory, a ghost from the past—a wraith skillfully sidestepping efforts to catalog.

Even the game itself remained to be identified—and for that he would seek the help of Honest Abe Weiss, the unconscious player. And perhaps, in the process, a serpent would be uncovered.

He punched the bell and waited while melodic chimes sounded patriotic notes deep within the rambling structure. Footsteps approached instantly and the door was opened a crack by a Chicano houseman. Bolan pushed the door fully open and stepped inside to the guy's spluttering protests.

There was a cool entry foyer sporting potted cacti, a low-ceilinged hallway dividing the structure with heavy Spanish doors to the left and right, an atmosphere of solidity and wealth.

"Message from Kaufman," Bolan snapped at the houseman. "Tell 'im."

The guy was torn with indecision. "The senator doesn't like to be—"

49

"Tell 'im!" Bolan snarled, adding to the discomfort.

The houseman's unhappy eyes gave it away, flashing uncertainty toward a closed door on the right.

Bolan shouldered the guy aside and let himself in. It was a large, plush den, decorated with antique guns and stuffed hunting trophies. An oval doorway at the far end led to a secluded dining area—breakfast room, maybe—with double-doors opening onto a shaded patio.

The senator was having a late breakfast on the patio, newspapers from several major cities stacked neatly on the table at his left hand. His was a face known around the world—hard blue eyes glaring fiercely through steel-rimmed glasses, that stern jaw and prominent chin, the shock of iron-gray hair neatly adorning the handsome head.

The guy did not look like a Jew.

He looked like a Nazi stormtrooper.

That famous chin thrust itself toward the intruder and those dissecting eyes crackled as the familiar voice demanded, "What the hell is this?"

The breathless houseman inserted himself between them. "He crashed in, sir. Do you know him?"

"He will," Bolan said coldly. The gaze rested fully on the senator. "The message is urgent, Weiss. Tell the guy to get lost."

A shifting of senatorial eyes was all it took. The Chicano disappeared. Bolan dropped into a chair and crossed his legs, casually settling in.

"It better be good," Weiss growled.

Bolan lit a cigarette as he replied, "It's not. Ike Ruby is dead. It's a war. They hit Moe's place,

50

too. Luckily, he wasn't there. But they took his kid."

The unreadable face turned in famous profile as the eye contact was broken. There was no other readable reaction. After a moment, the eyes still averted, that voice known around the world inquired softly, "Why are you bringing this to me? I'm not a policeman."

"Come off it," Bolan replied quietly.

"Who the hell are you?" Weiss asked, still not looking at him.

Bolan introduced himself with a marksman's medal, dropping it with a flat metallic ping on an egg-smeared plate.

Then the guy looked at him. Searchingly, coldly—more curiosity than anything else showing in that harsh gaze.

"So," he said simply.

Bolan said, "I think you may be next on the hit list."

"Let's talk about it," Weiss said, the voice coldly cautious but giving nothing. "Maybe we can come up with, uh, an accommodation."

Bolan's grin was pure ice. "Wrong reading," he said. "It's not my hit list. I think it's Bonelli's. And I think you need a friend."

The guy was quick. "Meaning you?" he asked, coming right back with it.

"Wouldn't that be ironic?" the Executioner said quietly.

"I guess it would," replied the senator who had been demanding Mack Bolan's scalp for lo these many months in the hallowed halls of congress.

"Don't let it worry you," Bolan said. "I wouldn't kiss you, Senator, with Augie Marinello's dead lips."

"So what are you doing here?" the guy asked tightly, cold hatred in his gaze.

"Looking for handles," Bolan replied truthfully.

"You won't find any on me."

"Puppets don't have handles," Bolan said. "Strings are the usual controls, aren't they?"

"You son of a bitch, you—get out of here! Who the hell do you think . . . ."

The anger spluttered off into rigid self-control. Those sky-blue eyes receded behind slitted lids— and, for a moment, Bolan thought he caught a glimpse of the Arizona viper in its native lair. The guy took a deep breath and asked his visitor, "Okay, what's your game? What do you want here?"

"I want you out of the game," Bolan replied coldly.

"Fine. Be assured, I want the same. Now get out of here. I'll give you a ten-minute head start before I call the police. But that's my final offer."

Bolan chuckled with ice on the teeth. "Here's a matching offer. I'll take Bonelli out if you'll take Kaufman."

"You're insane."

"No more than you. Maybe I don't fully understand the game yet, but I think I'm beginning to. And I believe that you are the prize."

"I'm the what?" Weiss snapped.

"The name of the game is *Puppeteer*. And you, Mister Righteous, are the prize puppet. Bonelli will own you or he'll take you out and put in one of his own. How does that sit?"

It was not sitting too well.

"You say they tried to hit Moe?"

Bolan nodded. "Pure luck saved him. He was out at a time when he is usually always in. Like you, Weiss, he's a man of vulnerable habit. They'll get him. Bank on that."

The guy had already banked it. "If what you say is true . . . ."

Bolan made a disparaging sound and replied, "I didn't risk walking in here to trade nothing but insults."

"But my God! This is ridiculous! It's crazy!"

"Who ever called them sane?" Bolan said quietly, referring to the Bonellis of the world—a meaning not lost on his listener. "If they want you, they'll have you. You signed it all away yourself, Weiss, when you gave it to Kaufman. You've been fair game from that moment. You're a piece of property, a chunk of meat to be owned and traded and sold on the open market. And Bonelli has decided to take you."

"We'll see about that," the senator replied stubbornly.

"*You* see about it," Bolan said, rising to leave. "But your only out is to go public. Ruin yourself politically. That would sever all the strings. Then you could call your soul your own. And I doubt that you'd draw more than a year in one of the federal country clubs. I hear life can be pretty nice there. You could write a book, make a fortune."

He was moving off.

Weiss called after him, "Wait a minute—wait! Let's scratch backs. I can be a good friend to have. I can make things a lot easier for you. Get that fucking wop off my back and you can write your own ticket with me."

Bolan paused in the doorway to send a withering gaze along the backtrack. "I should live so long," he said quietly and put that stench behind him.

He'd given the guy honest counsel—but then, of course, puppets were not particularly renown for standing alone. That one back there would not even contemplate the thought, nor had Bolan thought for a moment that he would.

He had the guy wired for sound, though, and he knew also that Honest Abe would lose no time seeking reassurance from the puppeteer.

Back in the warwagon, Bolan immediately summoned the wires on Abe Weiss, activating the surveillance system for simultaneous recording and live-monitoring. He got there in time to pick up and record for future reference several different telephone numbers as the senator searched via Ma Bell for his friend and political benefactor.

Weiss struck pay dirt on the fourth try. "I've been looking all over for you. What's happening?"

It was Kaufman's voice in the return. "Don't use any names. Keep it cool."

"Right, sure. God's sake. What is it? Are you laying low?"

"Sort of, yes. Listen, you better do it, too. I've been thinking about calling you. It's heat from the south, I think. I don't know what the hell it's all about, but you better cool it until I find out. Don't—"

"Dammit that guy Bolan was just here!"

"What?!"

"Yeah! I'm afraid that—"

"Say nothing else! Hang up, hang up!"

"Wait! I think he's on our side! It's the wops he hates! We could use the guy!"

"Hang up, dammit. I'll send you some comfort. Don't call again!"

Kaufman's voice was replaced by a loud hum. Weiss swore softly into the line and also hung up. Bolan was about to turn off the live monitor when another distinct *click* signaled the presence of a third party on that line.

So. Bolan's wires were not the only ones in Phoenix. He thought he knew, now, where to find Moe Kaufman.

He sent the warwagon tracking toward Paradise, homing on the corrupt connection that bound the state of Arizona in political slavery. He would sever that connection by whatever means necessary. And—no, Sharon—no promises at all.

CHAPTER 7

CONVINCERS

It was a rambling spread in the Old West style, complete with barbed-wire fencing and livestock grazing on the north forty. It was not exactly a "home on the range," though. A sprawling ranch house blended rustic architecture with tennis courts and an olympic-size pool, shiny patios, and gleaming lawn furniture.

The "retreat," yeah—a place where a harried businessman could get away from the pressures of the city and play at ranching with minimum discomfort.

Bolan's intelligence also suggested the Paradise Ranch as a clandestine center for illicit enterprises in both the political and commercial spectrums. The joint had all the appearances of a hardsite, for sure. Innocent-looking sentries in working western garb restlessly roamed the perimeters in jeeps and on horseback. "Workers" were spotted at strategic points about the lush inner compound surrounding the house. In the inner circle, hard-looking guys occupied tense positions at poolside—a human screen for the center of it all, the old master landlord of Arizona, Moe Kaufman. It was a conference of some kind, for sure. Kaufman, in swim shorts and terrycloth jacket, lolling on a sunning board with an upraised knee clasped in both hands; three younger guys, incongruously clad in business suits, occupying folding chairs in a semi-circle at his feet. It was a parley, all right. A portable telephone sat on a small table at Kaufman's left hand. He'd used it twice during the brief eyeball surveillance, on both occasions speaking animatedly and with obvious anger.

The warwagon was parked on the reverse slope of a shaded knoll overlooking the "ranch." The range was about 1,000 yards, elevation perhaps fifty feet, situation beautiful. Bolan sat on the forward slope in the shade of a gnarled tree, a wireless extension to the warwagon's mobile phone at his knee, the Weatherby .460 with sniperscope across his lap, powerful binoculars resolving the vision field an almost eerie arm's length away. He put down the binoculars to give naked eyes another panoramic sweep. The ranch stretched away from his position almost like a miniature set, Mummy Mountain in the distant backdrop.

Satisfied, finally, that the time was right, Bolan sighed and picked up the telephone.

He got a breathless pickup on the first ring. "Ranch."

"Put 'im on," Bolan growled.

"Who's calling?"

"Avon, dummy. Put me through."

A silence denoting some hesitance, then; "Okay. Hold it."

Bolan held it, raising the binoculars again to zero in on a movement at the patio door. A guy in shirtsleeves, calling over to the congregation at poolside.

Bolan panned across with the binoculars to pick up Kaufman in a moment of irritation. Heavy lips poured forth staccato response to the summons from the house even as a chubby hand moved toward the portable phone. Bolan smiled as he watched the emperor of Arizona delicately handle that instrument as though it were a bomb set to go at some undetermined moment, jowly face wobbling with thinly disguised tension. But it was the same houseman's voice that broke the silence across that connection. "Who's calling?" The guy again inquired.

Smiling grimly, Bolan spoke for the benefit of those ears at poolside. "I have news of Sharon. If he doesn't want to hear it, fuck 'im."

He indeed wanted to hear it. Breathlessly; "Okay, I'm on, let's hear it."

"The kid's okay," Bolan growled.

"How do I know that?"

"Because I say."

"Okay. I'll accept that for now. Get this, though, and be sure you understand it. If I find that girl with a hair out of place, I'll scorch this goddamned state from border to border, and I'll have balls and all of every sonovabitch involved in it. Understand that. I'll deal to get her back. But, man, she better get back smiling and happy."

"Relax, she's already back," Bolan growled.

"What?"

"You heard it."

"She's home safe? Who is this?"

"Nothing of yours is safe, Kaufman. For the moment, though, yeah, she's okay. I left her in her own hands and walking free. Do you know a kid lives over by the hospital?"

"St. Josephs?" the worried father replied quickly, then cautioned: "Say no more. I got it. Hey—I owe you. If this is level. What can I do?"

"You can listen for about thirty seconds and believe what you hear."

He watched perplexed eyes as they shifted rapidly in the magnification of the powerful binoculars, then the guy replied: "I don't—uh, who the hell *is* this?"

"The name is Bolan."

A sharp intake of breath was the only immediate response for the ears. For the eyes, a mixture of fear and disbelief filling the field of vision. Then, cautiously: "Convince me."

"Bonelli let paper on you. I sniffed it out and got there as they were leaving. They had your kid. I burned them down and sprung the kid. She's very pretty. Must have got it from her mother. Tried to convince me that her father is a poor misunderstood humanitarian with unfortunate business connections. But we know better, don't we? So does Bonelli. He wants what you've got, Humanitarian. You spoke of scorched earth, but it's all moving toward you. Can you believe that?"

"Maybe." The guy's eyes were working furiously, belying the calm of that voice. "Saying it's all true . . . what's your interest?"

Bolan gave him a chilled chuckle. "Come on, now. You know my interests."

59

"Are you looking for a connection?"

It was almost funny. Bolan told him, "I've found the connection. I'm going to sever it. Call this fair warning. Pull it in, Kaufman. I can't allow Bonelli to pull this off. If you don't make the cut, I'll have to."

Angrily: "I don't know what the hell you're talking about!"

Coldly: "Sure you do. You can have your little games on the home turf. If the people of Arizona don't care, why should I? But your Washington connections are a bit much—even for a provincial like you. For a cannibal like Bonelli, it's unthinkable. I can't allow it."

The guy was all but frothing at the mouth. "*You* can't allow it!? Who the hell—you wise shit!—where the hell do you get off—how the hell do I even know who's talking!?"

"Sever the connection, Kaufman. That's the only way you can save it, anyway. I'll take care of Bonelli. You take care of that Washington connection. I'll call it a successful mission and take my games elsewhere."

There was silence on the line for a long moment as the focal field of the glasses registered a full parade of conflicting emotions. Presently the guy sighed and calmly replied, "I still don't know you're who you say. And if you are, it makes no sense to me. Exactly what are you saying?"

"I'm saying I'll enforce the status quo . . . almost. Bonelli keeps Tucson. Kaufman keeps Phoenix but severs the national link."

Suspiciously: "And what does Bolan keep?"

Lightly: "Bolan keeps the peace . . . elsewhere. But you'll have to cut your national link."

"That's the game, eh?"

60

"That's about it. And it has to be quick. Before the sun sets again."

"What's the alternative?"

"You already said it. Scorched earth."

"How do I know this isn't—why should I believe a damn thing you say?"

"You need a convincer, eh."

"Damn right. Another thing, why should . . . ?"

Bolan set the phone aside and hoisted the big sniper to his shoulder. Eight thousand foot-pounds of bone-shattering energy would propel a heavy 500-grain messenger across that thousand-yard course in about one second flat. But the object, this time, was not to shatter flesh and bone. The object was to convince.

The pudgy racketeer sprang into sharp relief in the highly localized vision field of the big scope, fat lips still working in time with the crackling sounds emanating from the telephone receiver.

Bolan centered the crosshairs momentarily on that agitated mouth before tracking on. One caress of the finger at that moment would have stilled that forked tongue forever. But the pained face of a pretty girl streaked across the memory field, influencing an already reluctant trigger finger, pushing the scan onward. To take Kaufman at this point would be to play directly into Bonelli's designs on Arizona. Kaufman would keep.

The hairs were already calibrated to the range. A quick mental adjustment for windage moved them two clicks left of the portable telephone at Kaufman's side. No flesh stood in the path.

He squeezed into the pull and rode the recoil for instant target evaluation, smiling with grim satisfaction as that phone took sail in a flurry of flying fragments. The bullet got there faster than

61

sound, and Bolan was already squeezing into the next pull before that startled flesh down there understood what was happening. The hollow thunderclaps rolled away from his knoll across the flats to reverberate from the sounding board of the ranch house as puffs of cement dust and exploding glass marked the progress of the rapid-fire barrage, each round targeting harmlessly from the human point of view but wreaking considerable destruction upon inanimate objects.

No human flesh was in view down there, now. A couple of heads bobbed cautiously just above the surface of the pool. The sunning board was overturned; folding chairs scattered in hasty patterns of retreat. A jeep was tearing along a dusty road from the north forty, but there was no other obvious movement anywhere down there.

Bolan gathered his gear and withdrew.

Paradise Ranch had recognized a truth.

CHAPTER 8

THE WEDGE

The true scope of the Phoenix game was beginning to gel, imposing itself on Bolan's consciousness as a sinister silhouette, still devoid of detail, but already looming above anything he had been prepared to find in the Grand Canyon State. The Executioner had come to Arizona seeking heroin and dealers in the poison, but he had found instead that "something else," fragmentary, veiled, still incomplete, but *something*, something *big*, overshadowing the routine importation of Mexican drugs just as the Mafia itself overshadowed ordinary street crime. As that silhouette grew, expanding into a looming shadow of doom, Bolan realized the full urgency of his situation, his need to identify the game plan and the highly lethal players.

For once, the problem was compounded not by the usual shortage of leads, but by *too many*. Too many game trails to follow and too many players to identify without a comprehensive score card. There were simply too damn many fingers in the Arizona pie.

It had begun with Nick Bonelli, the Tucson Mafia, and heroin. Then came the startling realization of a secret paramilitary force drilling in the Tucson desert and striking northward toward the Phoenix preserves of Moe Kaufman and company. Complications aplenty, yeah. More than enough even before the addition of a kinky senator who was *maybe* being groomed as White House material.

Too many leads, sure. Bolan always sought the overall view, the *big picture*, but the picture in Arizona was just *too* big. The stage was so crowded with actors that the plot was all but lost in their entrances and exits. And the most recent addition to the cast was a face from the Executioner's own memory, an identity which eluded him with frustrating adeptness. Bolan had wracked his brain seeking a name to match that face, an identity to pair with that vague remembrance and the evil tremors it inspired. He had managed to eliminate known *mafiosi* and their hangers-on by scanning his mental mug file, which left him where? Vietnam? Before?

He brushed the phantom aside to concentrate once more upon the game itself, a mystery whose significance overshadowed the importance of any one man. Arizona offered so many opportunities for an industrious tribe of cannibals that Bolan scarcely knew where to begin looking. Heroin, sure, and all the associated border rackets which could rake in millions every year for the mob coffers. But Nick Bonelli *had* all that already, and he needed to prove nothing by declaring unnecessary war upon Kaufman and the Phoenix mob. The same argument negated consideration of the other routine rackets, which had been shared more or less peacefully by the competing mobs for over three decades. None of those rackets nor even all of them together could justify the expense and risk incurred by Bonelli in outfitting, training, and unleashing his private army.

And that left, yeah, *something else.*

Always the trail led back to Abraham Weiss, and politics, and . . . what? Real estate was booming in Arizona, and Bolan knew very well how deeply Kaufman and Weiss had mined the illicit goldfields of fraud and foreclosure. A land grab? Bolan put it down as a "possible" and continued his mental search.

Mining was important in Arizona, with the state supplying 54 percent of all American copper and one-eighth of the world supply. Silver and gold were big, too, and with them came the whole range of associated industries and manufacturing—electronics, aircraft, steel, aluminum, transportation equipment—the list went on forever. And much of that industrial wealth was centered around Phoenix. Of late, there had been rumbles up to the federal level about finding a suitable climate and industrial atmosphere for serious development of solar energy plants as an alternate fuel source for the entire nation. The Arizona desert had been suggested—by Senator Abraham Weiss among others.

And yeah, it might play. The Executioner's mind began to pick significant details from among the mass of useless ones, slowly shaping order out of chaos. Phoenix was already big in the Arizona economy, and by all indications it was slated to be bigger still, and very soon. And Phoenix belonged to Moe Kaufman in all the ways that mattered.

But for how long?

Bolan added up the possible ramifications of the deal, lopped off half for possible exaggeration, and still found himself looking straight at an impending *coup d'état*. The thought chilled him.

His hands clenched the warwagon's steering wheel, his jaw set in grim determination. A shattering offense was clearly indicated, but first he had to find the opposing team.

And where the hell were they?

"Is there any room for mistake?" Jim Hinshaw's voice was not hopeful, indicating that he knew what the answer must be.

"No chance, Jim," Angel Morales told him earnestly, to the accompaniment of Floyd Worthy's headshake. "I'm sure it was Bolan."

The black man softly added, "What did I tell ya?"

"Okay, okay." Hinshaw waved away the I-told-you-so's with an irritated gesture. "No sweat This is nothing we can't handle."

Worthy frowned. "We'd better get started then. We ain't done all that well handlin' it so far."

Hinshaw parried that verbal thrust with a question. "Why didn't you nail him when you had the chance?"

"You never saw a cat move that fast, man. Least *I* never did. He damn near *outran* those slugs from my '16."

"Don't build him up to be more than he is," Hinshaw cautioned.

"I'm not buyin' any ghost stories," the black man assured him. But that mother is *some kind* of man!"

"Some kind of *bastard*, you mean," Hinshaw countered. "I'm not the only one here with a score to settle with *Sergeant* Mack Bolan." He stressed the rank designation, turning it almost into an obscenity.

"We dig where you're coming from, man," Morales broke in. "But we can't play games with this dude. He's been tearing up the families from . . ."

"Save the history lesson, Angel. I did six months hard time thanks to that—" He left the sentence unfinished, the oath unspoken, but the grim set of his features told the story eloquently to his companions. Silence reigned in the office for a long moment before Hinshaw spoke again. When he did, all traces of tension and fury had been suppressed in his voice, and the facade of unshakable calm was restored.

"The mission comes first, as always. Bolan has involved himself now, and we have to deal with him as a definite threat. Angel, what did he want from Kaufman?"

The smaller man squared his shoulders before speaking. "Him and Kaufman were talking a deal, Jim. I swear to God."

Hinshaw was clearly skeptical. "It doesn't ring true. What's the scam?"

"Cease fire, so he says. If Kaufman cools it and takes out the Senator on his own, Bolan will take care of *us* for *him*."

Hinshaw shook his head as Worthy swore softly and said, "He just might do it."

"Not a chance," Hinshaw snapped. "We know the enemy now, and we can use that knowledge to advantage." He turned back to Morales. "Was Kaufman buying the truce?"

"He was thinking it over, Jim. He didn't say yes or no but . . . well . . . I think it's a go."

"So we play it that way. We can pull the rug while he's sitting on his hands."

"What about Bolan?" Worthy asked. "He won't be sitting on *his* hands."

"If we work it right, we can play them off against each other. While they chase each other around the block, we bag ourselves a territory. With luck they'll kill each other off. If not, we'll be waiting for the winner before he can catch his breath."

"How do you plan to run it down?" Worthy asked.

"We need a wedge, Floyd. Bolan offered the deal, so we have to play him up as the backstabber." Hinshaw thought for a long moment in silence. When he spoke again, his voice was firm with self-assurance. "Stay close to the wires on Kaufman and Weiss. I want to know every move they make *before* it's made. Everybody's on edge, and mistakes are inevitable. When they make one, we'll have our handle."

The other men grinned and rose to leave. Floyd Worthy paused in the doorway, turning for one final comment. "You know, man, if Kaufman can't put Bolan away, it's us against the sarge."

"I wouldn't have it any other way," Hinshaw told him solemnly.

Alone again, the soldier let his mind dwell on

the possibility of a confrontation with Mack the Bastard Bolan. A *second* confrontation, and the last one, too, one way or another.

Hinshaw's first meeting with Bolan had been long ago and thousands of miles away in another world and time. That meeting had brought the curtain down on the single sweetest experience of Hinshaw's life, cutting it off short. Not to mention the six month's stockade time and a less than honorable discharge, the only blots on an otherwise impeccable military record. Somebody had to pay for that disgrace. Somebody named *Bolan*. And Hinshaw had been waiting a long time to collect that tab. Waiting and hoping for another chance at Mack the Bastard. But lately, as he almost compulsively followed Bolan's campaigns in the newspapers and on television, his lust for the confrontation had begun to fade.

Wiping moist palms against his trousers, Jim Hinshaw wondered if Moe Kaufman would be able to take Bolan out. It would make everything so much . . . simpler, yeah . . . simpler and *safer*. He bitterly rejected the thought and its unsettling implications. He was *not* afraid of Bolan, dammit, he was just . . . *cautious*. Yeah, cautious. Everything that Hinshaw was or ever hoped to be was riding on this operation, not to mention Mr. Bonelli's money, time, and trust. Hinshaw had a duty to repay that trust with success.

Duty, yeah, you could never get away from it. Hinshaw fervently hoped that Kaufman would be up to handling the Bolan challenge, but a nagging apprehension grew in the back of his mind, setting his teeth on edge. *Us against the sarge.* Sure, and that would mean *Hinshaw* against Bolan.

"No sweat," he told the empty room, repeating it for emphasis. *"No sweat!"*

But he was lying to himself and he knew it.

Hinshaw's palms were moist again. It was a hell of a sweat.

CHAPTER 9

SUCKING

Mack Bolan was a supreme military strategist, his expertise acquired in the crucible of Southeast Asia. He had long ago learned that the best offensive tactic is seldom a wild-assed charge into the stronghold of an unknown enemy. Such *kamikaze* tactics might suffice on certain rare occasions but generally tended to be suicidal. Discretion often *was* the better part of valor, and the Executioner knew from practical experience that an overzealous enemy may sometimes be lured into a rash offensive with suitable bait. Invested with a false sense of progress, the enemy may be sucked to his doom in a prearranged ambush. The tactic was especially useful when the enemy was successful in camouflaging his base of operations, as Nick Bonelli's strike force had done so far.

Yeah, a suck play was clearly indicated. It remained only for the Executioner to choose the site and the bait.

The site was a shallow horseshoe basin on the western fringe of Echo Canyon Park, a miniature valley, really, bisected by a two-lane highway with lightly wooded hills on three sides. He parked the warwagon atop a shaded knoll on the left or northern tip of the horseshoe, nose toward the highway and rocket pod elevated. From his position he held a commanding view of the basin and the highway leading into it, ready to unleash his lethal firebirds on selected targets as they presented themselves.

Next on tap was the matter of bait.

He made the necessary call and again received instant pickup. "Ranch."

"It's me again. Put the man on."

"That was some damn fancy shooting, mister. Just a minute."

It was not a minute but a mere second before another instrument clicked into the line and Kaufman, very subdued, said, "Okay, you proved your point. We need to talk. Let's meet. You say where."

Bolan told him where, adding, "Ten minutes. If you're later than that, I won't be there."

"I can make that. I'll, uh, have some people with me."

"I strongly advise it. Bonelli has troops out scouring the countryside for you. You'd better travel heavy. But this is the way you do it. Two—"

"Wait a minute!"

"Shut up and listen. It's this way or no way. Two cars. Yourself and a wheelman in the first. A backup crew following at 100 yards. The second car keeps its distance."

"How do I know—?"

"Use your head," Bolan said disgustedly. "If I wanted it, I'd have had it instead of your telephone. I'm not your present hazard. Do we meet or don't we?"

"We meet," was the instant response. "Your way. But it better be cool."

"Ten minutes from right now," Bolan said and hung up.

It was a gamble, sure. Chancey as hell. A guy with Kaufman's resources could pull a lot of fancy strings in ten minutes. He could send police helicopters. He could probably field a makeshift force of forty to fifty men on a moment's notice, even should he elect to keep the cops out of it. And that was only half the risk.

He was gambling also on Nick Bonelli's field forces, practically certain that the telephone surveillance wires on Phoenix were Bonelli's wires but decidedly uncertain as to the number of guns in the Phoenix task force and their deployment.

It was purely an educated estimate that Bonelli could send no more than two or three cars to any point around the city with no more than ten minute's notice. If that estimate should prove wrong . . . then Bolan knew who could just as easily get sucked into this one.

It was possible, even, that he would be contending with two massive forces, one from each side of the set. And that could be curtains, for sure.

He had tried to foresee and to prepare for any contingency to the limit of his combat capabilities. But only the "meet" itself could tell the final tale.

He used the ten-minute wait for final preparations. The rocketry was "enabled" by electronic command, automatically superimposing the fire-

73

control system upon the optics, the electronic grid glowing red from the viewscreen.

From the console: *Fire Enable Go*

He set it up for manual command and made a slight adjustment to the optics, refining the focus, narrowing the vision field to a fifty-yard radius surrounding that fated slot on the desert floor.

Target selection, now, would be "gunner's choice." Wherever the optics wandered and settled, a simple bang on the knee would dispatch a firebird unerringly to the target centered there. Combat capability was limited to four birds, however. A reload would require sixty to ninety seconds at best—and many a battle had been lost in a single heartbeat.

But he settled into the wait with a satisfied mind. He had done all within his power to set the contest. The rest was in other hands.

He had chosen the site well. Not a vehicle strayed into the trap—not even a jackrabbit—when the thing began falling into place at minute eight. The first to enter was a speeding Continental—a burly, crew-cut man at the wheel, Moe Kaufman seated stiffly beside him. The optic system reached out at first contact to pull the vehicle into its resolving field, locked on, peering within to divine by long-range surveillance the true interior status. It was clean, straight.

Bolan punched back to wide-field surveillance, immediately picking up the trailing vehicle—a nine-passenger station wagon crammed with tense flesh, obediently maintaining a 100-yard separation behind the Continental. He localized momentarily to read the firepower in that wagon, then punched back to wide field to track both cars on into the slot. Kaufman was indeed traveling

74

"heavy." Bolan had read a couple of choppers, a long rifle with telescopic sights, and several shotguns among other armaments bristling from that crew wagon.

They were a minute early.

Both vehicles pulled to the side of the road at the designated spot. No one stood down. Both engines kept firing. After a moment, the Continental backed around to a position ten yards off the highway—poised perpendicular to the ribbon of blacktop, leaving the option open for fast take-off in either direction. Instantly, the station wagon did likewise. A couple of guys stood down, shielding eyes with the hands and craning the heads in nervous inspection of the surrounding terrain.

They didn't like it.

With good reason. It was the sort of place where wagon trains of old ran tautly at full speed in fear of red man ambush.

But it was perfectly to Bolan's liking.

Minute nine arrived, and, with it, another vehicle running swiftly into the focal field. But it was not the hoped-for Tucson task force. It was a pretty girl moving a small British sports car with the hammer down, long hair riding the wind inside that open convertible, face set in grim concentration. There was no time for Bolan to speculate upon the presence of Sharon Kaufman. Obviously she had followed the convoy from Paradise Ranch—perhaps arriving there just in time to note the hurried departure and opting for pursuit.

There was no time because a grimmer presence had also made an entrance into the set. It began as a dark mass at the extreme edge of vision, separating quickly under the probing focal finesse of the optics system into a four-car caravan, big black crew wagons running in close consort and closing quickly.

A quick pull-back to wide field showed Moe Kaufman stumbling from his vehicle and running with arms flailing toward the blacktop, galvanized by the unexpected appearance there of beloved flesh—the little sportster burning rubber and fish-tailing to a quick halt.

Another punch of the optics revealed the prime enemy in disturbing close-up. A black face there, eyes concealed behind dark glasses, lips moving rapidly in final instructions, a black beret perched jauntily at the side of the head. Another—lean and brown, narrowed eyes harshly scanning the terrain from the tail car. The rest of those faces were stereotypes. Bolan had seen thousands just like them. But those other two . . . yeah, it all flooded back, ghosts from the past, psychotic goons in army O.D.

Now he knew his enemy.

Another face from the same past should have been present also. That it was not brought a chill to the Bolan spine. Hinshaw was the name, canni-balism was the game—but cannibalism with a dif-ference—a *military* difference.

And now he knew that the die was cast. He'd sucked a bit more than he'd expected—and now Kaufman and his girl may have to pay the price for an Executioner's sloppy intelligence effort.

The hit team was speeding into the slot.

Kaufman's crew was now electrically aware of the "betrayal," scrambling for position and send-ing frantic signals across the 100-yard separation from their boss. Kaufman had the girl in tow, and the two were sprinting toward the Continental.

Bolan hoped the big vehicle was a "tank"—an armor-plated retreat—but it did not bear the telltale signs, and even that would not prevent disaster should the "betrayal" become a fact.

Mack Bolan was resolved that it would not.

He banged his knee when the charging lead vehicle was three lengths into the slot. An angry firebird lifted away with a rustling *whoosh* to sizzle along the target track on a tail of flame and smoke. He saw their flaring eyes in the vision field as the fiery missile closed—then flaring eyes and all disappeared behind a mushroom of roiling flames. The vehicle reappeared a moment later as it careened onto the desert, first kneeling then shuddering onto its crumpled nose and doubling back in an end-over-end barrel roll of disintegrating metal. The fuel tank caught the spirit of the thing on the third bounce and completed the destruction with a secondary explosion that littered the area with smoking flesh and shredded hardware.

Meanwhile, the closely following second vehicle discovered the hard way the hazard of running too close in a pack. At the moment of rocket impact, something had blown back and smashed the windshield of that second car, sending it spinning out of control along the blacktop and coming to rest on its side in a grinding slide almost to the doorstep of Moe Kaufman's outraged crew.

Automatic weapons fire immediately joined the cacaphony of doom, accompanied in concert by the basso booming of rapid-fire shotguns—and there was no comfort there for the survivors of that second pile-up.

Cars three and four were meanwhile reacting

in the only sensible manner, both of them peeling instantly away from the blacktop and jouncing across open country on widely diverging courses.

But Bolan had punched back to target focus and he had one of them in the range marks. The console sent him an immediate *Target Acquisition Go*. He thumped his knee and sent another terror. It rustled along the range and overtook the target vehicle, punching in from the rear and lifting the whole works in a thunderous plunge to nowhere. Two of Kaufman's boys immediately trotted off in pursuit to assure the fate of the occupants.

The fourth car from Tucson was executing a tight circle, careening along the reverse course in a desperate effort to regain the highway and put those hellgrounds behind them. Bolan acquired them on his grid, doubled fist poised above the knee, then he changed his mind and instead disabled the rocketry. The pod retracted and locked into place beneath the sliding roof panel. He sent a quick probe into the slot, saw that all was well there with the Kaufman camp, then instantly returned his attention to the fleeting prime enemy. He watched the wild fishtailing as some newly educated goons in O.D. found their purchase on solid surface and began the streak to safer ground.

Moments later, the warwagon was moving smoothly along the track, the optics maintaining "shadow distance" behind the remains of the retreating task force.

Bolan had not "spared" them . . . and they would never again find "safer ground."

"Take me home, boys," he said quietly to the optics monitor. "Let's take it all the way to hell."

CHAPTER 10

AUDACITY

Mack Bolan had first encountered Jim Hinshaw and his two sidekicks during his second Asian tour of duty. Their encounters had been rare, brief, and—for Hinshaw at least—very unfortunate. The last of those encounters had resulted in Hinshaw's brief imprisonment, and the less than honorable discharge of all three men. Bolan had known only part of it then, picking up bits and pieces as the court martial progressed, and the sequence flashed before him now as he tracked Angel Morales and his raiders toward their lair.

Hinshaw, Morales, and Worthy were lifelong natives of Tucson. They had become fast friends in grade school and remained so ever since, their interracial camaraderie a minor curiosity in a city whose schools were not entirely unfamiliar with ethnic antagonism. While other adolescents banded together for safety and sport in racially homogenous gangs, Hinshaw, Morales, and Worthy stood apart, dubbing themselves "The Desert Rats" and displaying a belligerent pride in their mutual alienation.

Fighting and rumbles were inevitable, and with them came a string of adolescent capers beginning with shoplifting and gradually progressing to car theft and assault. Through it all, Jim Hinshaw emerged naturally as the head of the tiny gang, the strategist and "brains" for a series of minor-league depradations. Worthy and Morales recognized Hinshaw's native craftiness and qualities of leadership, deferring to him without protest, accepting his counsel readily and generally profitting thereby. Hinshaw's operations were logically and meticulously planned, lucrative more often than not. Only the hot car ring had gone sour, and even that was a blessing in disguise, for it inspired Hinshaw's Rats to join the U.S. Army en masse one step ahead of nosy police investigators.

The trio from Tucson had enlisted and trained together, volunteered for the Special Forces together at Hinshaw's earnest suggestion, and arrived in Vietnam together as members of the same Green Beret A-team. Comrades and superiors found them zealous and adept at the martial skills, and then-Corporal James Hinshaw was especially singled out for praise concerning his selfless devotion to duty.

Those commanders had missed the mark there, badly misreading their man. For Jim Hinshaw was devoted not to duty, but to *power*. He lived for power, worshipping it as some men do their gods, lusting after it as other men do beautiful women. He cared not so much for money, though he never passed up an easy profit, recognizing material wealth for what it was, a means to an end and a *symptom* of deeper power and influence. To Hinshaw, power was an almost spiritual concept, the ultimate goal of all endeavor, the ability and *right* to impose order on the lives of lesser individuals. Floyd Worthy and Angel Morales understood their comrade and were content to board the bandwagon in subordinate positions, assured in the knowledge that Hinshaw's ultimate success would bring benefits to all.

Vietnam had been heaven on earth for Jim Hinshaw and his Desert Rats. Assigned to the Army's pacification program in Trah Ninh Province, operating out of My Hoi village, they immediately began taking stock of the local situation and its potential for manipulation by skilled hands. Shortly after their arrival, the sergeant in charge of Hinshaw's A-team was the single casualty of a midnight "guerrilla raid." The attackers were never identified, although troopers Worthy and Morales did bag three peasants near the camp an hour later, riddling them before they could escape—or surrender. Hinshaw was routinely elevated to the rank of sergeant, and the marksmanship of his friends was rewarded with commendations and, in Worthy's case, promotion to corporal.

Things began to change in Trah Ninh Province, as Hinshaw led his henchmen in the subtle establishment of a personal jungle fiefdom. Their commanding officers were naturally preoccupied with the broader conduct of the war, leaving the trio more or less free to institute a campaign of intimidation against inhabitants of the region. The Desert Rats gradually became a greater object of local fear than the Viet Cong, and the local peasants accepted their plight with a stoicism born of centuries-long oppression. That is, *most* villagers accepted it, although two village chiefs in My Hoi were assassinated by "unknown terrorists" before Hinshaw could install a leader of suitable pliability.

Then began the long night of Trah Ninh Province. Artisans, politicians, and eventually almost everyone was forced to pay "insurance" premiums to Hinshaw or face arrest on charges of subversion and involvement with the communists. Local girls and women were recruited and sold like chattel to whoremasters in Saigon, while a few were retained by Hinshaw for a local prostitution network of his own. Persons of every age and both sexes were forcibly enlisted as couriers of drugs and other contraband between villages and into neighboring provinces. Dissenters were rare, due primarily to the overabundance of lethal accidents which haunted the exponents of discontent. When Hinshaw's commanding officer responded to rumors of unorthodox proceedings in the province, he gained dubious distinction as one of the earliest victims of "fragging" in the Asian war. A black GI was observed running from the scene of the grenade blast, but no assailant was ever identified.

Disaster came to Hinshaw's personal kingdom in the person of Mack Samuel Bolan. Bolan had met Hinshaw several times while working the delta with Sniper Team Able and had considered him a competent, if unusually stern, soldier. His opinion changed drastically following a raid during which Bolan executed VC Colonel Tra Huong and two lesser associates in the south of the province. Returning toward their base camp outside

My Hoi, Bolan and Corporal T. L. Minnegas had encountered Hinshaw, Worthy, and Morales in the act of executing three unarmed villagers. One was already dead, but Bolan's intervention had rescued the others and resulted at length in the indictment of all three men on manslaughter charges. Villagers slowly and cautiously came forward with tales of coercion and violence, and other charges were added. Military prosecutors did their best, but matters were seldom clear in Vietnam during the late sixties, and the Desert Rats offered a vigorous defense, asserting their efforts were to stem Red aggression in the province, portraying their accusers as communist partisans. The final verdict was at best a compromise. Morales and Worthy escaped with less than honorable discharges, while Hinshaw was sentenced to six months in the stockade and a similar discharge.

Mack Bolan had recognized the vengeful bitterness in Hinshaw, but chose to forget it as the Asian war and a later, more personal one enveloped his life and transformed it into a never-ending cruise down Blood River. Now the shadows of the past had been resurrected, and much of what had only been confusion now made grisly and ominous sense.

James Hinshaw was an organization man, a master strategist backed by two guns as lethal as his own. Or rather, *one* other gun now, with Floyd Worthy a smoking twist of lifeless meat back there at the ambush site. Hinshaw with his team had been the perfect man to train and lead Nick Bonelli's private military force, a totally ruthless and amoral man whom the Tucson *capo* could count upon to serve the project with unswerving dedication and zeal.

A serpent, yeah, and a damned lethal one at that. A sidewinder.

Bolan tracked the hastening crew wagon north out of Echo Canyon Park, following Morales and his men as they swung west onto MacDonald Drive and skirted the limits of Paradise Valley. He was with them when they veered due south on 44th Street, pursuing discreetly but inexorably as they angled back toward the heart of Phoenix. The Executioner remained alert for any deviation from the track, dreading the confrontation to come if Morales should lead him back into the teeming center of the desert metropolis.

Bolan's silent prayer was answered. The crew wagon chose an intersecting desert highway, nosing eastward in an apparent effort to complete a perfect rectangle with its progress. Bolan gave them a lead, then resumed the track, driving on by as the limo swung onto a graveled access road and faded into a screen of dust.

The Executioner sought a parallel track and found it a quarter-mile further on. A mile from the paved highway he was able to pick out buildings off to the side, and leading to those structures, the plume of dust trailing Angel's vehicle. Bolan found his own track circling slowly toward the distant cluster of houses and followed it gratefully, homing on what he knew to be the viper's nest he had sought since entering Phoenix.

Bolan left the warwagon where his route intersected a sagging barbed-wire fence, completing his cautious approach on foot. He circled the dry, rolling terrain warily, Big Thunder and the

84

Beretta Belle ready for action at right hip and left armpit. No man opposed his penetration. Judging from the known body count in Phoenix and a mental sizing of the barracks at the Tucson hardsite, Bolan estimated that close to two-thirds of Hinshaw's force had been eliminated. He hoped to confirm that estimate by direct observation preparatory to any penetration of that armed camp.

He found a low ridge 100 yards from the cluster of buildings, with desert sagebrush and stunted trees combining to offer adequate concealment for his purposes. Prone amid the thorny vegetation, Bolan scanned the compound with his field glasses, taking in the reception for Morales and his surviving raiders. Counting Angel and his crew, there were eleven heads down there, hardmen all, milling about the dusty crew wagon and peppering the new arrivals with demands for information.

And Jim Hinshaw was present and accounted for at the heart of the miniature mob scene, questioning Morales, and not at all happy with the answers he was getting. Bolan could not hear what Hinshaw was saying, but he could read plainly that furrowed brow and the grim set of the mouth. The guy was anything but happy, but he seemed to be maintaining control of his temper. As always, control and order were Hinshaw's watchwords. Even when Hinshaw resorted to torture and murder, it was done methodically, devoid of emotion.

Cool as ice . . . and deadly.

Bolan's eyes narrowed as he watched Hinshaw lead his shrunken hardforce into the largest of three buildings. The man was a menace, his lethal potential compounded by the almost phlegmatic precision he brought to every endeavor. Whatever the end goal of the Arizona game plan, Jim Hinshaw was the man who could carry it off.

Unless he was stopped . . . totally and permanently . . . cut off at the knees by a superior force.

Bolan scanned the buildings and grounds through his glasses, noting relationships and proportions, angles and planes. The largest and central building was probably Hinshaw's command post, with space reserved for quartering at least some of the troops. The function of the other structures was open to surmise, but the tall radio antenna erected beside one of them gave Bolan a clue to its primary purpose. He felt safe in assuming that he had found the nerve center behind the "ears" in Phoenix . . . the alert and deadly head of a serpent whose heart lay to the south in Tucson.

A penetration was indicated. More, it was mandatory at this stage of the Executioner's Phoenix campaign. The suck play had now fulfilled its purpose by leading Bolan to his ultimate target in the desert city, and he meant to strike against that serpent's head before the brain could recover from earlier stunning blows to marshal a venomous counterstroke.

Bolan was formulating his strategy as he turned away from that arid tableau and retraced his steps to the battle cruiser.

An effective strike would require an effective penetration—and that could be tricky with a pro like Hinshaw. But Bolan was not going for a simple hit-and-run, he was hoping for the knockout—a quick one-two—not just to the head of this beast but to the entire fetid structure.

That would call for a bit of audacity.

Audacity, hell, he had plenty of it.

CHAPTER 11

THE MESSAGE

Hinshaw's voice was tense, taut—dangerous. "From the top, Angel. What went sour?"

"It all went sour, Jim," Morales replied with a disgusted gesture. "I think it started sour. It was a suck play straight from the jungle book."

"You said a rocket attack?"

"Yeah. They sucked us into a horseshoe slot, then layed into us from the high ground. There was no way to save it. I'm damn lucky I got out. Poor Floyd . . ."

Hinshaw kicked the desk and raised his eyes to the ceiling. "Bastard!" he growled. "He must have tumbled to the telephone tap. How cute. Did you eyeball the bastard?"

The little Latin shook his head and said, "All I eyeballed was them damn rockets whooshing down from the heights. He's got some kind of

fancy firepower. Forget them fucking LAWs—
this was big stuff. More like guided missiles."

Hinshaw muttered, "So he's teamed up with
Kaufman."

"Looks that way," Morales quietly agreed.

"You know what this means."

"Yeah," Morales said, sighing. "And we're running about 70 percent casualties as of right now,
man."

"So what are you reading?" Hinshaw growled.

"I'm reading scratch," the surviving lieutenant
replied. "We can't pull it now. Not without reinforcements anyway."

"You ready to tuck your tail?" Hinshaw asked
heavily, "and slink back to Tucson? You ready to
face the old man with that?"

"You should've seen what I faced a little while
ago, Jim. Listen. That guy deserves his reputation."

"So does Bonelli," Hinshaw said worriedly.

"Well, shit." Morales threw up his hands and
walked nervously about the room waving them as
though seeking applause from some invisible au-
dience. "This is crazy. I say we call out the hole
card and tell them all to go to hell."

"Not yet," Hinshaw said. He gnawed on his
lower lip for a moment, then added: "We can still
pull it out, maybe." His eyes gleamed with silent
speculation, then: "There's a million bucks on Bolan's head. Right?"

"You know *why* the bounty is a million?" Morales inquired quietly. "It's a million because the
meanest guys in the mob haven't been able to
take the guy. That's why. I wish you'd been out
there with me awhile ago. I wish you had."

"He's just a soldier," Hinshaw mused. "What the hell, Angel . . . he's *just* another soldier."

"Go tell that to Floyd and B Troop," Morales replied bitterly.

"With a cool million on his head."

"Shit."

The debate was interrupted by a knuckle rap at the door. A squad leader poked his head in to report, "We got company." His gaze flicked to the window. "You better see."

A big guy in Levi's was standing outside the fence, jawing with a sentry.

Hinshaw turned from the window to scowl at the squad leader. "What is it?"

"He walked in. We spotted him about three minutes out. Walking the phone line. He says we got trouble. Do we have trouble?"

Hinshaw picked up the telephone, listened to it for a moment, then put it down and said, "Yeah. Sounds like eggs frying on there. Dammit! No wonder I got no—how long has it been out?"

The squad leader shrugged. "I didn't know it was until the guy came along."

"Okay, let him in," Hinshaw growled. "Make sure somebody sticks with him. Give the guy a beer. He looks hot and bothered."

"Shit it's about a hundred out there in the shade, if you can find shade," the squad leader commented. He went out muttering, "I wouldn't have that guy's fucking job on a . . ."

Morales was standing at the window, silently gazing out, hands stuffed into his pockets. "What d'you suppose a job like that pays?" he said with quiet reflection. "Couple hundred a week?—maybe two-fifty?"

90

"You thinking of joining up?" Hinshaw asked heavily.

"Look at the guy. Probably been out there all day in that heat. For what? Tell me for what, Jim."

"Maybe he lost his nerve," Hinshaw pointedly replied. "Maybe he never had any. How 'bout you? Ready to trade it all for a timeclock and a pile of bills?"

"Hell no," Morales said quietly.

But he remained at the window and watched "the telephone guy" go about his little duties. The guy went up the pole, carrying a bag of tools and crap with him.

"What a dummy," Morales commented softly. "Can you beat it?"

"We're doing it, aren't we?" Hinshaw replied. "We're beating it. Right?"

Morales turned around with a grin. "Sure, man. We're beating it."

"Go keep an eye on the guy, huh? Just for safe? I have to call old man Bonelli."

"You're forgetting the phone."

Hinshaw chuckled. The tensions were gone. Angel was back and they'd pull it out together . . . somehow. "We're going to collect that million, Angel. *Us*. We're going to bag a bonus baby. Go watch the dummy. Let me know as soon as the line is restored. I need a parley with our noble benefactor in south Arizona. I want him to get his bank ready."

Angel laughed and repeated his little applause routine as he headed outside to keep an eye on "the dummy."

But that dummy, be sure, was no dummy.

"The dummy" now stood on a little ridge far removed from but overlooking the base camp. He'd gone down there and rubbed shoulders with the enemy, sampled their iced beer, played games with their telephones, traded a couple of tall stories while getting their numbers and reading their strengths and weaknesses—and closing the adventure on a note of amost ludicrous melodrama.

Angel Morales had tried to recruit him.

It had been a deft try, full of veiled promises while devoid of job description—but certainly a recruiting pitch to anyone "in the know" and able to decipher the doubletalk. Bolan played dumb and, in the process, bought himself enough time to complete the mission in proper fashion— thanks entirely to Morales.

Of course, in all fairness to the guy, Angel Morales had never actually "known" Sergeant Mack Bolan. They had crossed gazes a couple of times in 'Nam but that had been a long time ago; also, since then, Bolan had undergone surgical alterations to the facial structure to the point where a close friend from the old days would pass him by without recognition.

Still, it was quietly satisfying to Bolan that he could successfully penetrate a professional camp. There were no false illusions regarding the expertise and military capability of men such as Hinshaw and Morales. Renegades, right—but soldiers still, and they had trained in the same classrooms as Mack Bolan, had survived the same hazards of combat. And it was not contempt for the enemy which provided Bolan with confidence enough to successfully penetrate; it was a recognition and understanding of the complex mental processes which allow *identification.*

With that understanding, Bolan had early become a master at what he termed "role camouflage." Often he had been totally isolated deep in VC territory, his freedom and survival dependent on wits alone. He had survived many such entrapments. Once he had donned a standard black poncho and an appropriated coolie hat to kneel for hours beside a narrow stream, "mending" abandoned fishermen's nets in the midst of an occupied village. Somehow, even in such an alien environment, Bolan had always seemed to "belong" to any scene to which he lent himself.

Variations upon the same theme had served him well throughout his personal war against the Mafia, always to their disaster.

With a bit of luck, this time, renegade soldier James Hinshaw would fare no better from a walk-in visit by Mack Bolan.

His "tool kit" for that penetration was in reality a mobile munitions lab. And he'd gooped that joint for destruction from end to end, despite the watchful attentiveness of his hosts. Plastics with time-delay fuses were left at a critical point on the outer wall of the communications hut, tamped to blow inward—hopefully to buckle the wall, drop the building, and topple the mast for the radio antenna. Another application would level the barracks; others were placed for strictly psychological effect.

And that was but one side of the "knockout" equation. The other side was psy-war all the way. Bolan was hoping to stage a master illusion which would confuse and divide the enemy toward their ultimate destruction. Not just here in Phoenix, but back at the heart of the operation as well.

The "psy-war" equipment was now being emplaced. And it hurt the warrior's soul to contemplate the loss of such a fine weapon—but then, weapons were expendable. Human freedom and dignity were not.

Head weapon was the slick M2 .50-caliber heavy-barrel machine gun. He set it gently upon the sandy soil of the ridge and threw off the cover. Sixty-six inches of sleek death machine, the M2 was the most lethally impressive weapon in Bolan's mobile arsenal. Tripod-mounted, the heavy gun would deliver at the rate of 650 rounds per minute from a muzzle velocity approaching 3,000 feet per second. No flesh—and few vehicles or buildings—could stand before that withering stream of big steel-jacketed slugs.

And this one came with a difference—one of armorer Bolan's own devices.

He emplaced the big weapon with care, adjusting the tripod legs and sighting-in for maximum effect. Then he locked in the ammo box and fed the disintegrating-link belt into the weapon's receiver. Two steel rods went into the earth, emplaced nine inches to each side—swing-stops, positioned for a desired 45-degree arc. He rotated the weapon to verify the arc, then completed the sighting, making fine adjustments for range and azimuth.

Finally he affixed the "difference"—a boxlike device designed to fit over the butt and grips of the M2, a spring-loaded metal tongue meshing with the trigger assembly. A simple timer surmounted the metal box. Bolan consulted his watch, set and wound the timer, and activated it.

Psy-way, yeah.

If all went well, those guys would think themselves involved in a very hot firefight, precisely

150 minutes from that moment. The planted plastics and the robot gun would do their things together. In the heat and hysteria of the moment, who would know between timed-explosives and another "rocket attack."

To complete the stage dressing, Bolan strewed throwaway fiberglass tubes from several expended LAW rockets about the emplacement. Anyone who'd ever handled an M2 would not be fooled for long by the little charade, but Bolan was not going for longs; he would be content with an early confusion among hot tempers and shaken combat instincts.

Somehow, he had to either equalize or destroy the warring factions in this state—and he had to do it damn quick. He was sitting duck on the desert and he knew it. Plenty of combat stretch, sure, but damn little comfort in the "withdraw and retreat" department. Any concerted and determined reaction by the police community would be his undoing for sure.

"Damn quick" was the name of the game in more ways than one. He had to cover nearly 200 miles of desert highway between Phoenix and Tucson damn quick. He had to do it in the convincing neighborhood of 150 minutes. And by God he would. He summoned all the horses from the big Toronado power plant and headed for Interstate 10.

The Executioner had to deliver a message.

Not to Garcia, no.

It was a message that only a Mafia boss would understand . . . loud and clear.

CHAPTER 12

SYMBOLS

Nick Bonelli hit the roof, as expected. But the Tucson *mafioso* was a cat, adept at landing on his feet and not yet ready to surrender the last of his nine lives. Plans had gone awry before, but the world was still turning, and Nick Bonelli was still around. Sure he was mad—mad as hell—when the soldier boy called from Phoenix with his tale of twenty dead men and no visible progress. Who wouldn't be mad as hell? But on second thought, after careful reconsideration, Bonelli realized that the setback to his military arm might be a blessing in disguise. It was Nick Bonelli's chance to get in on the action personally.

He had relished that possibility from the start. Oh sure, he had gone along with his son Paul on the idea that the Phoenix move should be made by an outside force, not readily traceable to the brotherhood. And that soldier, Hinshaw, had been the only logical choice. Tough. Hard as nails. And smart, too, don't forget that. The boy had brains to spare. "Combat sense," Paulie had called it. A good choice, yeah.

But Nick Bonelli missed the action. He secretly longed for the excitement he used to feel in the old days, riding the beer trucks with Tony Morello and the other old boys. Most of them were gone now, one way or another, but Nick was still around. And he needed action.

Besides, he had a personal stake in the Phoenix game plan. It was no mere lust for action that spurred him on now to take personal command of the compaign, but rather a matter of inner necessity. Too much was at stake up north for the *capo* to just sit back and watch it slip away with a wistful sigh because some soldier boy got caught with his drawers down.

Personal, yeah.

For years—hell, for *decades*—Bonelli had watched with ill-concealed jealousy and spite as Moe Kaufman and Ike Ruby pulled the strings of power from Phoenix, while he, Nick Bonelli, a brother of the blood, sat on the sidelines and champed his bit. The California bosses, Julian Di-George and Ben Lucasi, had forged close ties with Kaufman while paying lip service to their alliance with Bonelli and growing rich at his expense on one-sided narcotics deals. Or so Bonelli described it to himself, although each kilo of Mexican brown had fattened his bankroll considerably. Even Augie Marinello, and through him *La Commissione*, had smiled upon Kaufman's Phoenix clique when it should have been Bonelli at the helm in Arizona. It was Bonelli's *right* as a brother of the blood.

Of course, Nick had tried to rectify the uneven situation over the years, peacefully at first and later by force. He had opened a posh nightspot in the heart of downtown Phoenix, seeking thus to establish a beachhead, to drive home a wedge that would pry the town open for full-scale invasion. The results were humiliating. At Kaufman's orders, teams of local police stationed themselves outside Nick's place every night, checking the age of customers and making spot arrests for public drunkenness. Nick wisely withdrew that probe.

Next he tried assassination. Twice, teams of hardmen drove north in search of Kaufman and Ruby, and twice, they disappeared without a trace. Rumors circulated of midnight funerals in the desert. Johnny Scalise, Nick's own cousin, volunteered to fulfill the contract and hurried up to Phoenix. Johnny did not disappear. A carload of Boy Scouts found his nude and emasculated body, crucified with barbed-wire bindings to a giant roadside cactus.

Matters had rested there until Paul Bonelli had approached his father with the news that he not only knew the way to get Kaufman, but he also had the man to do it. From there it was off to the races, with Nick funneling men and cash into Hinshaw's hands, preparing for the big push into Phoenix that would knock Moe Kaufman off his stolen throne.

Paulie and Hinshaw had suggested that Kaufman might better serve the cause alive than dead. Bonelli had resisted the idea as anathema to his inbred sense of revenge, the vendetta. But at length he came to realize the wisdom of their words, for Moe Kaufman alive could serve well as a puppet on Nick Bonelli's strings. Kaufman had the connections already, let him continue to retain the appearance of power, as long as he knew in his heart where the *real* power lay. It could all be so satisfying, rubbing Kaufman's nose in the muck and stripping him of his empire, leaving him alive to grieve over the loss of that which he could never regain.

Satisfying, yeah. And rewarding. *La Commissione* could hardly fail to recognize the power and tactical brilliance of the man who could execute such a masterstroke. At last Nick Bonelli would be assured the respect of those old fools who had snubbed him while courting the favor of Kaufman and his connections. And the plan had shown every sign of working out smoothly. Hinshaw's men were primed and ready, poised to strike at Kaufman's jugular and apply the pressure that would bring him to his knees. Everything should have gone like clockwork.

Mack Bolan changed all that.

Bonelli had secretly expected a visit from Mack the Bastard for a long time. He thought that time had come when the guy stopped off in Arizona long enough to kick some ass with Ciro Lavangetta and Johnny the Musician, but it turned out he was only passing through on his way to Miami. Bolan had done Nick a favor there, for Ciro had died in Miami, severing the encroaching tentacles of the old DiGeorge family onto Bonelli territory. But Nick had always known that Bolan would— indeed, *had to*—come back.

In spite of that mental preparedness, that back-of-the-mind alert, Bolan's appearance *now* had caught Nick completely by surprise, threatening to louse up everything that Bonelli and Hinshaw had been working toward for months. Bolan anywhere in Arizona was bad news, but Bolan *in Phoenix* could be unmitigated disaster, the absolute *worst*.

Or maybe not.

After the first panic reaction had faded, Bonelli took stock of the full potentials of the present situation. Hinshaw assured him that Bolan and Kaufman would be at each other's throats before nightfall, and the soldier seemed confident that given a few hardy reinforcements, he could play both ends against the middle. Bonelli had sent the reinforcements, almost gleefully, despite the half-hearted tongue lashing he had given Hinshaw on the phone. Maybe—just maybe—Bolan's arrival could be *good* news for the Tucson *capo*. There was that cool million still riding on the guy's head, and Bonelli could always use that kind of money. But more enticing was the mammoth prestige that would automatically fall upon any man who could bag the Executioner's head. And if Nick could bag Bolan *and* Kaufman at the same time, with a made U.S. Senator as the kicker—well, Bonelli just had to smile at the prospect, his mind conjuring images of himself as the new man of the hour. Boss of Bosses? *Capo di tutti capi?* Why not?

He fired a two dollar cigar and reached for the desk intercom. His house boss, Jake Lucania, appeared in answer to the bleeping summons.

"Get Phoenix on the phone, Jake. I need another parley with Hinshaw."

Lucania answered, "Sure boss," and went to place the call. It had been over two hours since Bonelli's last contact with Hinshaw, and more than an hour and a half since Paulie had pulled out with a war party. Bonelli was sending reinforcements all right, and he was sending his son and strong right arm as well, just to insure that there was no more dicking around.

Minutes passed, and then Lucania reappeared to announce: "He's on line two, sir."

Bonelli nodded a silent thanks and scooped up the receiver, greeting Hinshaw with a curt, "What's happening up there?"

The younger man's voice sounded defensive, on edge, and maybe just a bit nervous as he answered. "No change, Mr. Bonelli. My—we're sitting tight like you suggested."

"Okay. Paul is on the way with some help. Look for him any time now."

There was a long pause, and when Hinshaw spoke again, the note of tension and suppressed resentment in his voice made Bonelli smile. "I understand, sir. As you wish. But I honestly feel that I—"

"It's no disgrace to need help, kid. You been hurt bad. Paul can give you a lot of comfort. How many boys you got left there?"

"Roughly a dozen, sir. They're all in top form, and I'm confident that with the replacements you've sent we can save the play without further difficulty."

"Yeah, great," Bonelli answered, though certain in his own mind that there would be a great deal more difficulty before the final curtain came down in Phoenix.

Hinshaw was muttering more assurances when Bonelli broke in again. "Listen, about this Bolan thing—"

Bonelli's words were cut off by a curious hollow booming sound at the other end of the line. It filled his ear, stabbing painfully into his brain, and the line was suddenly buzzing, with Hinshaw in the background loudly demanding to know what the hell that was. The sounds from the Phoenix end became jumbled then, with a second explosion and a third coming almost together, and the loud thunking sounds which Nick Bonelli, the old street warrior, identified at once as heavy-caliber bullets ripping through walls and furniture. Hinshaw and company were catching hell in Phoenix, and Bonelli could do nothing but sit there and listen to it happen.

And then, suddenly, he could not even do that. The line went dead.

But no, it *couldn't* be dead. He could still hear the sounds of battle, the staccato gunfire and booming explosions. They sounded the same, and yet different at the same time. Sharper somehow, and clearer. *Closer.*

Nick Bonelli rose from his chair and bolted for the study door as the floor beneath him lurched in another blast. The rattle of gunfire was loud in his ears now, and there could be no possible doubt as to its meaning. Lucania burst through the door at that precise instant, a thin trickle of dark blood bisecting his ashen face.

"It's a hit," he shouted at the would-be Boss of Bosses. *"We're being hit!"*

Bolan had pushed the warwagon hard, urging unaccustomed speed from the Toronado engine and reaching his target in western Tucson with minutes to spare. Nick Bonelli's fortress home lay there, almost on the fringe of Rolling Hills golf course and backed against an arid river bed called Pantano Wash. Bolan made a quick drive-by, pressing the appropriate button on his command console to trigger the "collection" of data from miniature recorder-transceivers previously installed on the Bonelli phone terminals. The taped data was pre-edited and time phased, omitting wasteful periods of silence to present an uninterrupted flow of intelligence. The playback was running as Bolan prepped for combat, enlightening him as to the latest troop movements and reassuring him that the *capo* was at home within those walls.

He stowed the warwagon in a screen of willows along Pantano Wash, on the northwest flank of Bonelli's hardsite, and immediately enabled the rocketry, aligning selected points of the manor house and fortifications in the range finder of the firing grid and registering the coordinates in the memory bank. His touch upon a special set of controls meshed the computer and firing mechanism, setting the rocketry on "automatic." He set the console timer two minutes ahead and quit that vehicle, the sounding of the lethal metronome loud in his ears.

The Executioner moved swiftly over the arid ground, despite the tremendous load he carried. Along with the Automag and Beretta, extra clips and grenades girding his waist, he carried his big double-punch weapon, the M-16/M-79 combo. The autoloading assault rifle could spew 5.56mm tumblers at a rate of 900 rounds per minute, while the 40mm hand cannon slung underneath was a single-shot breechloader, handling tear gas, buckshot or HE rounds at the discretion of the gunner. Satchels filled with clips for the M-16 and mixed rounds for the grenade launcher completed the Bolan combat rig, upping his normal weight by some seventy-five pounds.

He did not seem to feel that weight or be affected by it as he scaled the stony wall and put himself inside Bonelli's estate. He moved swiftly across the rolling expanse of finely manicured lawn, making no effort at concealment while his mental alarm clock ticked off the numbers until doomsday.

The first hardman saw him at fifty yards out. Obviously unable to believe his eyes, the guy just stood there and gaped for about a half-second too long. When he made his move, simultaneously squawking a warning and reaching for his sidearm, the effort was too little and too late. Bolan's finger stroked the trigger of the M-16 and the guy went into a jerky little dance of death. The gunfire alone would have alerted the whole compound, but it was instantly eclipsed by the sound of hell arriving to visit the ungodly.

Bolan had glanced at his watch and saw the sweep second hand signal doomsday. Over his left shoulder, then, came a faint *whoosh* from the warwagon's rocket pods as the thunderbolts came in directly on time and on target, rattling over the low defensive wall at three-second intervals. Number one erupted at the front gates, shattering those portals and flinging the debris of stone and humanity about like so much flotsam on a raging sea. Number two impacted between two limousines parked in the curving drive, lending shreds of blackened steel and streamers of flaming gasoline to that lethal atmosphere. Numbers three and four had been reserved for the manor house itself, and they plowed in as ordered by the warwagon's electronic brain, unleashing a volcano of flame and oily smoke within that palace of corruption.

Men were milling around that funeral pyre like

ants in a bonfire. They were shouting and brandishing weapons, but confusion reigned supreme and no man seemed certain where to go or what to do. The Executioner helped to resolve that fatal uncertainty, sweeping the ranks with a prolonged burst from his automatic rifle. Guys were flopping around down there, wallowing in their own juices and shrieking as the spray of steel-jackets ripped through them. Those still standing spun toward Bolan and flung ineffectual pistol fire in his general direction.

He emptied the clip of the M-16 into those stumbling, staggering straw men, then slammed a fresh clip home and emptied that one as well. Unsatisfied, he gave the M-79 its roaring head, alternating rounds of buckshot and high explosives as he marched a parade of death across those hellgrounds.

A handful of walking wounded were frantically dragging themselves toward hopeful cover.

Bolan let those survivors go, turning his attention to the house itself. It was burning now in spots, sagging badly in others where the deadly firebirds had impacted in their flight, but the overall structure stood defiantly, a symbol of all that Bolan had sought to eradicate in Arizona. He turned the grenade launcher on that castle of gloom, spewing round after round of explosives and gas into the smoking shell. Masonry flew. Bricks showered the grounds, punching holes through the pall of smoke in their passage. Secondary explosions sounded within the bowels of that structure as a plume of inky smoke rose straight into the cloudless Arizona sky.

It was enough.

The message was loud and clear.

Bolan poised there for a long moment surveying that scorched landscape, the stench of gunpowder and blasted flesh irritating his nostrils, then he spun about and went out the way he'd come.

The old man may or may not have survived that holocaust. Either way, the message was sent and received. There would be no easy take-over in Arizona . . . not this time.

But the real battle still lay to the north. Bolan was strongly aware of that fact. He'd monitored the telephone conversations, knew that fresh troops were being rushed to the combat zone, knew that plenty of hellfire and thunder lay in his future.

The presence of people such as Hinshaw and Morales in this environment of corruption constituted a clear and present danger unimaginable to the average citizen. A natural rapacity combined with military expertise and further combined with the greed and power lust rampant in the area could spell nothing but death and dishonor to the people of Arizona.

So no one had appointed Mack Bolan their lord protector. So what?

So the common man in the street looked on underworld hoods as some sort of glamorous, charismatic defiers of the system. So what?

Bolan was not there for applause, nor was he there to save Arizona from itself. He was there because his destiny was there, because he could not turn away from his fate.

He was an instrument of an evolving universe.

He was Judgment. Not the judge, not the jury, not the sentence itself.

Mack Bolan was the Mafia's *Judgment* . . . and he knew it and accepted it.

Let the people of Arizona accept what they would.

CHAPTER 13

FACE

"It's hard to believe one man could do all this."
Paul Bonelli was fit to be tied. His narrowed eyes
scanned the compound, lingering over various
points of particular carnage.

"Well, one did," Hinshaw replied, a defensive
tone edging his weary voice.

The two men stood on the porch of Hinshaw's
field headquarters. A handful of Hinshaw's men
flanked their leader, remaining aloof from the
forty or so Tucson hardmen milling around their
crew wagons in the yard. Bonelli's gunmen were
taking in the incredible scene as well, commenting
on the site's condition in hushed tones.

There was much for comment. The walls of the
main building were riddled with symmetrical
holes, the window frames splintered and empty
except for jagged shards of glass. The ruined hulk
of a limousine slouched beside the house, its

pock-marked body sagging to starboard on two shredded tires. Behind the ventilated structure, two mounds of blackened lumber memorialized the former existence of other buildings.

The younger Bonelli shook his head in bewilderment and turned toward the door. Hinshaw got there first, holding it wide for the Tucson underboss. Bonelli accepted the courtesy as his due and stepped inside, pausing briefly in the doorway to finger the jagged splinters left by heavy-caliber slugs which had punched through the wooden panel. He took in the interior damage at a glance: walls scarred by bullet gouges, furniture overturned and shattered.

"How many did you lose this time?" he asked Hinshaw.

"Four dead, two wounded. It's a wonder we didn't lose more."

"Any rumbles from the cops?"

"None. Neighbors are scarce around here. And they mind their own business."

Bonelli nodded his satisfaction with the answer, allowing his eyes to sweep the room again. His gaze settled on a large weapon which sat atop a dusty tripod in one corner of the room. Two short tubes made of plastic or cardboard or something were propped against the big gun, completing the sinister little tableau. The *mafioso* gestured toward the pile of weaponry with one hand as he turned toward Hinshaw.

"That's it?"

"That's it. A .50-caliber machine gun and a couple of LAW rocket tubes." Hinshaw's tone was brisk, matter-of-fact.

"What's that LAW?"

"Light anti-tank weapon," Hinshaw explained

to the "civilian." "Think of it as a throw-away bazooka. We found them on a rise overlooking the compound, about a hundred yards out. He did this with the fifty," Hinshaw's hand swept the room, indicating the hundreds of bullet holes. "It has an automatic trigger lock, set for continuous fire. That left his hands free to handle the LAWs."

"The chopper shoots by itself?" Paul Bonelli was skeptical.

Hinshaw nodded. "It's a relatively simple mechanism. He probably—"

"Simple?" Bonelli interrupted, scarcely able to believe his ears. "It was simple for *one man* to kick hell out of your entire force? What were your *boys* doing, Jimmy?"

"Dying," Hinshaw answered flatly. "Or trying like hell not to."

Bonelli was boiling. "It looks bad, Jimmy. One guy dumping all over—how many men is it now?" The Tucson sub-*capo* knew very well how many men had been lost before Hinshaw answered "twenty-three" in a tired voice.

Bonelli nodded solemnly as he repeated the number aloud. Then his tone softened and he took a different tack with the beleaguered field commander. "Okay, I can see what you've been up against here. I understand. But my papa, now . . ." Paul left the sentence hanging, letting Hinshaw know that Don Niccolo Bonelli was not apt to share his son's understanding of the situation.

He let Hinshaw think about that for a moment, then added, "I hate to bring home news like this so soon after your other troubles." Another pause, then, "Maybe I don't have to tell him right now. I guess we can wait until after we have this thing in the bag." Bonelli smiled at the scowling soldier. "We *are* going to bag it, aren't we?"

The telephone rang, breaking the tension building there. Hinshaw seemed frozen for a long moment, then reluctantly scooped up the receiver.

"Hello? Yes, hang on." He held out the instrument to Bonelli. "For you."

Paul accepted the receiver and growled into the mouthpiece. "Yeah?"

The voice at the other end of that connection was taut, breathless. "Paul? Jake Lucania here."

"Yeah, Jake."

Lucania's words came in a breathless rush. "We been hit! You never saw such—it's—I mean—"

Bonelli shushed the excited flow. "Jake! Relax now and take it from the top one time."

Lucania was still breathing heavily, but more slowly now as he answered. "Okay, right. I'm sorry. We been hit. The house is mostly gone, and we lost more'n a dozen boys."

"How is he?" Bonelli asked, knowing it was unnecessary to speak his father's name.

"Oh, he's okay. Shook up some, mad as hell. He told me to call you right away."

"Who hit you?"

"It was Bolan for damn sure."

Bonelli's eyes floated toward Hinshaw. "For sure, eh?"

"As sure as can be. Half a dozen boys got a look at him. A big stud, all in black, guns and shit hangin' all over him. It was Bolan all right, or else he's got a twin."

"There's no twins," Bonelli said grimly.

"Yeah, well . . . ."

"When was this, again?" Bonelli asked worriedly, still looking at Hinshaw.

"It was exactly, uh, twenty-five minutes ago."

"That's very interesting."

"Listen. He wants you back here. Right now."

"Tell him I said he should button up tight. We got a situation here, too. I'll get back as soon as I can. But I gotta . . . I'll call you back, Jake." Bonelli broke the connection and turned to face Hinshaw with a hard look.

"When did you say you got hit?" he asked quietly.

"Hell, I told you. It was just before you arrived."

"I been here about ten minutes."

"Yeah. Well . . ." Hinshaw stretched to his toes and gripped the back of his neck. "So I'm surprised you didn't run into the guy on your way in. The attack lasted, uh, say three to four minutes. It was hit and run. Time we got unglued and started a reaction, the guy was gone. Go put a hand on that M2. It's probably still hot."

"You got hit about half an hour ago, then."

"Give or take a minute or two, yeah."

"Bullshit."

The soldier's eyes flared. "Huh?"

"Bolan was hitting our ranch about half an hour ago, give or take a minute."

"That's impossible," Hinshaw replied softly.

"Tell papa it's impossible. The guy leveled the place."

"Then Bolan didn't do it. He was—"

"I said bullshit," Bonelli cut in coolly. "They saw the guy. It was him. He was 200 miles from here at the time you say you got hit."

Hinshaw's face darkened. "What d'you mean I

112

say I got hit!" His hand made a dramatic pass of the room. "What the hell do you call *this*?"

"I can see what it *looks* like," Bonelli said curtly. "Now I'm asking you what really happened."

The scowling Hinshaw quickly replied, "Are you calling me a liar, Mr. Bonelli?"

The Tucson underboss did not miss the sudden formality. "Simmer down," he said. "Nobody's calling names. I'm just saying you got it wrong. You read it wrong. Now, I'm saying, you need to read it again."

The military chief lit a cigarette and turned toward a shattered window. Presently he turned a musing gaze toward Bonelli and said, "Okay. I'm reading it again. I told you the M2 was rigged for autofire. Even had a sweeper on it. I think we been had by some fancy footwork. I think the guy *was* in both places at the same time."

Bonelli shook his head. "Try again, Jimmy."

"It could be done. I don't know how those LAWs could have been programmed for . . . but— well hell, come to think of it, how do we know he even used LAWs. He could have . . ."

"You're trying too hard," Bonelli said coldly.

"The guy got inside somehow. He came in here and set it up."

"Save it!" Bonelli snarled.

"I don't like your insinuation!" the soldier yelled.

"Fuck what you don't like," Bonelli growled. "Your problem now is to give me something that I might like!"

"Dammit, it's a Bolan hit," Hinshaw fumed. "It has his signature all over it. The guy came in here and set us up. Then he zipped down to

113

Tucson and timed it for a simultaneous one-two. He's trying to drive a wedge between us, trying to fragment us. We used that tactic all the time in—"

"I said save it!" Bonelli cried angrily. "Don't serve me that kind of shit!"

A seemingly genuine expression of new revelation crossed the soldier's eyes. "The phone man," he said, sighing.

"What phone man? Make it better than last time, Jimmy." That was a threat, directly stated.

Hinshaw either did not hear or he let it pass. "The son of a bitch," he said, the voice awed. "He waltzed right in here, drank our beer and . . ."

"What, *what*?"

"You wouldn't like this, Mr. Bonelli," the guy said, very quietly. "It would scare the shit out of you. Let me handle it—just forget it and let me handle it."

"You're getting paid to handle it," Bonelli said coldly. "Try cute games with us, though . . . ." It was another threat, this time received and understood.

The soldier's eyes flashed angrily, but there was no further reaction. Bonelli took a final look around, squared his shoulders, and walked quickly out of there.

That soldier could lose more than his face this time. He could, yeah, lose his whole damn head.

Hinshaw watched Paul Bonelli go with mixed feelings of anger and apprehension. Tension coiled within him like a cold fist clutched around his heart. For the first time, he feared that he was really losing control in the Phoenix game, and he didn't like that feeling. Not even a little bit.

Hinshaw had not been happy with the news

that Bonelli junior was leading the reinforcements to Phoenix. Except for two things, he
would have opposed the move. Number one, by
the time he had learned about it, the troops were
already on the road with Paul in command. And
number two, it was distinctly unhealthy to buck
Nick Bonelli when his mind was made up, even on
small matters. On a matter as all-important as
this one, such opposition would undoubtedly be
fatal.

Well, Paul Bonelli was there now, and Hinshaw
did not for one moment buy that business about
the guy just being there to "keep an eye on the
boys." Bonelli was there to keep an eye—and a
tight rein—on *Hinshaw*. From the minute he
stepped out of that shiny Detroit tank, Paul
Bonelli was in command of the Phoenix game,
and everybody concerned knew it. Whatever
sugar coating Paulie or his father tried to put
on it, Hinshaw was being relieved of his command in all but name, and the idea rankled him.
And yet, if that had been all there was to it, Hinshaw might have been content to roll with the
punch, biding his time.

But there was more, much more going on in
Phoenix than a Mafia warlord expressing dissatis-
faction with a field commander. Hinshaw didn't
know for sure yet just what it was, or even who
was pulling the strings, but he could feel his
hackles rising as they had in 'Nam, when some
sixth sense had warned him of impending ambush
by the Cong.

Jim Hinshaw was being set up. But for what?
And by whom?

If Mack Bolan was pulling the strings, there

was nothing Hinshaw could do except try to anticipate the next blow and brace himself for it when it fell.

Things might be different, though, if the setup was a Bonelli operation. There just *might* be some-thing that Hinshaw could do to prepare for *that* eventuality. Something decisive, maybe.

Hinshaw picked up the phone, which had done so much to derail his schemes of late, and quickly dialed a local number. He recognized the answering voice and got down to business without wasting time on preliminaries.

"Get the men together on the double. I'll expect them to be ready to move within twenty minutes. Can do?" He acknowledged the affirmative reply with a terse grunt and broke the connection.

Hinshaw was calling up his reserves. He had not been green or foolish enough to enter the Phoenix campaign with only thirty men at his disposal, nor had he been inclined to place himself at the mercy of replacements from the south. Like any field commander worthy of the name, he had trained and positioned a secondary force in anticipation of unforeseen setbacks . . . from *any* faction. The "hole card," as Angel called it.

Jim Hinshaw did not intend to lose face—or anything else—from this operation. It had been recognized from the start as his golden opportunity to establish himself as a man for the world to reckon with.

He would *not*, dammit, return to the obscurity that had held his manhood captive through all those drab years.

He was going to bag himself a bonus baby, all the damn Bonellis to hell. And he'd walk over

116

39

anybody to get Mack Bolan's head in a sack.

He'd have it, dammit.

The cute bastard. New face, eh?

All faces looked the same inside a paper sack.

CHAPTER 14

LINKS

"I'm not asking you, I'm telling you!" Moe Kaufman's voice was angry, betraying signs of the inner strain which had dogged him throughout that day. "I need protection. *Now!*"

He sat in a richly panelled conference room upstairs in the Phoenix City Hall. Facing him across the broad table were two command-rank officers from the city police department and a captain from the county sheriff's office. The lawmen looked unhappy, their faces wearing almost identical expressions of grim displeasure and embarrassment. Their eyes alternated between the tabletop and Kaufman's face as the mobster continued his harangue.

"I put you guys where you are today, don't forget. And I expect some return for my investment. I made you and I can *unmake* you just as easy."

Frank Anderson of the Phoenix PD spread his

big hands in a placating gesture. "C'mon, Mr. Kaufman. There's no reason for these threats. We're doing everything we can to—"

"Bullshit!" Kaufman snapped, watching the officer redden. "You haven't done a goddamn d thing except haul a few stiffs to the coole. and stake out the places the guy's already been!'

"It's standard procedure, sir," the sheriff' captain interjected.

Kaufman turned to him with a glare. "This is not a standard situation, Joe. You're not running some punk gamblers out of town to make the department look good at election time. This guy s after my ass! He could shake the whole damned thing apart!"

The officers were silent, waiting for the outburst to run its course. Kaufman slumped back m his padded chair and took several deep breaths, regaining his composure before speaking again. "I want some men with me day and night. Fix it."

"Policemen?" Frank Anderson sounded uncomfortable.

"Why not? I'm an upstanding citizen whose life has been threatened by a known maniac. What better cause do you need? Log it as a Bolan stakeout."

Anderson nodded slowly, clearly unhappy about the situation. Kaufman didn't give him time to brood about it. "I want men on Weiss, too," the mobster said.

Again the desultory nod.

"Okay." Kaufman was partially placated. "Now fill me in on what you've accomplished toward bagging this psycho Bolan."

"First off," the sheriff's captain said heavily, "we don't read the guy as being a psycho. He—"

"Save it for the eulogy," Kaufman snapped. "What are you doing to stop him?"

The police spokesman took over. "We have SWAT teams on standby alert around the clock. Roving patrols everywhere we feel he's likely to surface—that is, around *your* places." A glare from Kaufman killed the guy's grin as it began. "Okay, uh, the chopper is up and in full communication with the ground patrols. On the federal level, we have liaison with the local FBI, and a planeload of U.S. Marshals in due in any time. Some kind of special Bolan strike force."

Kaufman said, "Okay. Maybe it's finally getting off the ground." He paused, then continued, "I want all of you to remember above everything else that this guy is bad for business. My operations are at a standstill, and I'm sure I don't need to remind you that *your* monthly take depends upon *mine*. The longer Bolan runs loose in this town, the worse it is for all of us. And if he gets *me*, you can all kiss those nice fat envelopes goodbye."

Anderson sighed and said, "I can detail a pair of plainclothes officers to you, and a couple for Weiss. Any more would bring the headhunters down on me from Internal Affairs."

"How soon can I have them?"

"They'll be waiting when you get downstairs."

"Good." Kaufman rose to leave, pausing as he turned from the table to reinforce his earlier message to the three men. "I want this Bolan, you understand? I want him dead! Pass the word that there's a bounty of five G's on the bum's head. Maybe that'll sharpen somebody's shooting eye."

The three officers rose to usher Kaufman out. Anderson offered his hand, but the mobster brushed past him, eating up the corridor with brisk, energetic strides.

Yeah, five grand should buy a little unaccustomed alertness from the boys in blue. Kaufman almost smiled as he felt the old familiar stirrings of power which had always exhilarated him. It made him feel good to have men indebted to him here, in the halls of goverment. Also, Bolan wouldn't shoot back at cops—that much was well known—and if they could manage to corner the guy, he would be a sitting duck, as good as dead. And if they couldn't trap him? Well, the guy never stayed long in one place, and the extra heat would surely hasten his departure. He'd blow town before long, maybe heading south to mop up Bonelli and the Tucson crowd. So much the better. All Kaufman had to do was go underground, stay safely hidden behind his cops, and ride out the storm. Later, when all the clouds had blown away, he could surface again and resume business as usual. There might even be thoughts of a punitive excursion southward, if any foes remained alive there.

Kaufman was almost chuckling to himself as he reached the elevator—not that there was anything in particular to laugh about, but things sure looked a lot better than a few hours ago. Sharon was in good hands, now—safe and sound. A grin did tug the heavy features a bit as he thought again of that walloping at Echo Canyon. He had to give credit to that young man—psycho or not, he carried a hell of a punch.

The Phoenix boss reached the elevator station and extended a hand toward the call button. Another appeared from nowhere to cover the button—a big, muscular hand with powerful fingers and a heavy wrist.

The man who had materialized behind him said quietly, "Not yet, Kaufman. You owe me a parley."

God, it couldn't be! Not right here in the damn police station of all places!

But it was, obviously, Mack Bolan. Psycho, no—indeed not. Those eyes were hard and full of ice, but they were the eyes of a man who knew himself.

"What a hell of a nerve," Kaufman muttered. "One snap of the fingers and you're up to your neck in bluesuits, mister."

"I'm ready to die if you are," the guy said in that curious warm-cold voice. "Snap away. But I'd rather parley."

And parley they did. Right there in the damned police station.

Bolan was playing it straight, clad in a light-weight denim suit and soft shoes, unarmed, entirely vulnerable, gambling more on the happy fates than on any good faith on the part of Morris Kaufman. He steered the guy to an empty office, closed the door, and told him, "It's out of hand now. Paul Bonelli and forty Tucson torpedoes hit town awhile ago. They came for blood and they'll damn sure get it. So our deal is off. I wanted you to know. Figure I owe you that much, though I'm damned if I can say why."

The guy's eyes flared a bit at the news, but he was no sob-sister. "The deal was never on, was it?"

"I guess it wasn't," Bolan agreed soberly. "How's the girl?"

"She touched your heart, eh?""

Bolan allowed a brief smile. "I still have one, yeah."

"She's okay, thank God. She told me how you bailed her out this morning. I'm indebted. But only so far. You've decided to turn tail and run, huh? Doesn't sound like the things I've heard about you. I guess legends are like that."

"I guess so," Bolan replied. "But you misunderstood me. I'm hanging around. To pick up the pieces."

Kaufman's eyes again flared. "What does that mean?"

"It means I play the only option left. Bonelli will take you, that's certain. But he'll suffer a bit in the taking. Maybe enough that I can take him then."

"That's your option, eh?"

"That's it."

"You didn't risk coming in here just to tell me that."

Bolan smiled again. "No."

"You tried to set me up at Echo Canyon, didn't you? Then Sharon blundered in and your heart just wouldn't allow it. You had to pull it out. I'll have to say, it was a hell of a pull." The guy shivered slightly. "I get goosebumps just remembering it. But okay—bygones are bygones. I have another option for you. Are you listening?"

"I'm listening," Bolan assured him.

"You take Bonelli out. Then you write your own check and I'll sign it."

Bolan grinned and told him, "You're offering coals to Newcastle, Kaufman. I shake the mob's money tree any time I please. I don't want your money."

"What then? You name it."

"I already named it," Bolan replied casually.

The racketeer's face darkened. "That's unreasonable. Abe Weiss and me go back a long ways. Why're you so upset about poor Abe? Hell, all those guys owe their souls to somebody. How the hell do you think they ever get the office? Don't be naive. Politics is just another form of business. It's no better and no worse than any other business."

"Stop," Bolan said quietly, "I have a delicate stomach."

"Do-gooders," Kaufman sneered. "The world is weary of guys like you. Why don't you open a church?"

"Why don't you?" Bolan countered. "Take Sharon as your first convert. Tell her all about the new nobility and baptize her in whoredom, heroin, and innocent blood. Then ask her to kneel down and worship you as much as she worships you right now."

Surprisingly, to Bolan, it got to the guy. His eyes fell and he clawed for a cigar to cover the emotion.

"That was a low punch," he muttered.

"Truth is like that," Bolan replied quietly.

"Get outta here," Kaufman said, just as quietly.

"A final word, first. Your only out is via Weiss. Cut your losses, guy. Cut that bastard loose and send him to Siberia or somewhere equally cool. Let him live out his days with memories of what he might have been—except for you."

"I can't do that," Kaufman said in a barely audible voice. "Now get out of here before I suddenly lose my mind and start yelling for a cop."

124

"He's your Achilles' heel," Bolan said. "It's better to lose the foot than the head."

He walked out and left the guy standing there in contemplation of his feet. So much for the "Kosher Nostra."

Bolan had already written the guy off. He was so much dead meat, no matter what course of action Bolan may follow now. But a stubborn sense of rightness had sent the Executioner into a pursuit of that "parley"—a certain "combat honor" which was as important to maintain as the mission itself. And Mack Bolan had become known throughout the underworld for the sanctity of his word in dispensing those rare battlefield agreements or "white flags" to his enemies.

And, yeah, maybe also the Bolan heart had been touched just a bit by a loyal young lady who would hear no evil concerning her father.

Well, he'd tried.

Now the whole thing was in cosmic hands.

He returned to his battlecruiser and pointed her toward the next link in the chain. As he pulled away, another vehicle entered the late-afternoon traffic and fell in behind him. He caught the maneuver immediately in the rearview but lost interest when the possible tailcar fell back and turned away. There was too much to occupy the combat mind now, to cloud it with vague worries.

But, sometimes, a little cloud changes the perspective. Bolan should have worried more.

CHAPTER 15

ONE MORE TIME

Abe Weiss had gone hard.

A vehicle with an alert wheelman was parked across the road from his driveway, and a guy with "gun" stamped all over him was loitering beside the hedges inside the yard. Another, no doubt, would be inside somewhere.

Bolan went on past and pulled into a service area a half-mile down the road—service station, small restaurant, fast-food grocery. He pulled on the shoulder rig, tested the action, and dropped a spare clip into the coat pocket as he pulled it on.

A few cars were parked at the restaurant, several more in front of the grocery. He activated the security system and locked the cruiser, then walked into the service station office. Two cars were at the pumps—one headed east, the other west. A guy with greasy hands moved in from the garage area to give Bolan a questioning look.

He flashed a police ID wallet at the guy as he told him, "I broke down. They're sending a wrecker, but I have to get into town fast. Get me a ride, huh?"

The guy frowned, said, "Sure," and went out, wiping his hands with a gas-soaked rag. He went directly to the westbound car and leaned in from the passenger side to make his pitch. Instantly he straightened and made a hand signal. Bolan strolled out, gave the guy a sour, "Thanks," and slid in beside the accommodating driver—a nervous man of about fifty wearing horned-rim glasses and a business suit.

" 'Preciate it," Bolan told the motorist with a flick of tired eyes.

"My pleasure, officer," the guy said quickly.

They sat in strained silence while the servicing was completed. As they pulled onto the road, the guy timidly inquired, "Should I put the hammer down?"

Bolan showed him a genuine grin as he replied, "No hurry. Actually I'm only going a half-mile or so. I'll tell you where."

It was a very sedate half-mile journey, almost like a driving test—and just as strained. He stopped the guy directly opposite the stake-car, thanked him, and sent him on his way.

The wheelman in the hardcar was giving plenty of interest. Bolan called over, "Relax, it's cool," and walked up the drive.

The yard man was on him immediately. Bolan had the ID wallet ready. He flashed it and said, "You're relieved. Beat it. Take your boys with you."

"I don't understand," the guy said, but obviously he did.

"He's getting an official detail. You won't want to be here when they arrive. Go on. I'll baby-sit him until they get here."

The guy started to say something negative, then checked it and substituted: "I got a man inside, that's all. Maybe I should phone first."

"And maybe you'd like to be here when the Secret Service boys arrive," Bolan said quietly.

"Oh! I see, yeah, I get what you mean."

The hardman spun about and went quickly to the house, Bolan right behind. The door opened to their approach and another torpedo stepped outside.

"Feds are on the way," the crew boss explained. "We're leaving. This guy's a cop. It's his worry now."

The inside man shot Bolan a glowering look as he moved past. The two went quickly along the drive without a backward look. Bolan waited until the vehicle pulled away, then he stepped inside the house and shot the bolt on the door.

Honest Abe was in the hallway, about six paces in, a Browning pistol at the unwavering eye level.

Very coldly, Bolan suggested, "Use it or lose it. Right now."

The senator hesitated for several heartbeats, then slowly lowered the weapon, turned away from the confrontation, and stepped into the den. He was at the desk when Bolan entered, the Browning at his fingertips, hard eyes giving nothing to the unwanted visitor.

"Sort of sad, isn't it," Bolan said softly. "A United States senator, a prisoner in his own home, skulking around with a boomer in his hand."

"I know how to use it," Weiss snapped, putting

the intruder on notice. "I could have given you a third eye just now."

"I've heard about your kills," Bolan acknowledged, his gaze flicking across the stuffed trophies which decorated the walls. "Somehow it's different, isn't it, when the prey is looking back at you ... or if there's a possibility, he could start shooting back."

"It wasn't lack of nerve, Bolan. What do you want?"

"Same thing," Bolan replied. "I want you out."

"You should live so long. Save my time and yours. Get out of here and mind your own business."

Bolan let out a long stage sigh and went to the window, turning his back to the man with the Browning, offering him a target, almost hoping he'd try it. He did not. Bolan turned back toward the desk and said, "I'm afraid you are my business, Senator. We can save the whole country a lot of pain. Put it down. Get out ... while you can. I just came from a parley with Kaufman. The feeling—"

"Don't try to snow me," Weiss snarled. "I heard all about your desert rendezvous with Morris. Your fireworks dazzle me not at all. And I am not particularly impressed by perfidy."

"Look who's speaking of perfidy," Bolan replied calmly. "The most traitorous son of a bitch ever to sit in the United States Senate. You're a national disaster, Weiss."

Taut muscles jumped in that granite jaw, but the guy did not rise to the bait. He smiled nastily instead and said, "This morning I was a puppet. Now I'm a traitor. You're not a very good fisherman, Mr. Bolan."

129

"Who's fishing?" Bolan asked casually. "I know what you are and you know what you are. The question is, what will you be tomorrow?"

"I'll still be here," the senator said with a glassy smile.

"Wrong," Bolán quietly told him.

Weiss snorted.

"You'll be in an unmarked grave at Paradise Ranch."

That brought a reaction, just beneath the surface of those steely eyes. "Bullshit," the senator said.

"It's his only out. He's setting it up right now. It's called cut and run, Senator. You understand the terminology. It's the opposite of stonewalling."

"Get out of here, Bolan. My patience is gone." The hand was hovering above the Browning. "And I patently dislike cat and mouse games. Especially those at the kindergarten sandbox level."

"See," Bolan responded softly. "You *do* understand. You'll be buried in a sandbox, Weiss." He walked casually to the door, again offering the guy a broad target, then turned back to say: "Remember me to the fallen angel. And don't forget that I told you first. Keep that Browning cocked and close. Why do you think the bodyguards left?"

That one struck close. Weiss stood up, the head cocked slightly, eyes working furiously. "I forgot to ask," he said in an almost conversational tone. "How *did* you get rid of them?"

"I brought them a message they couldn't refuse."

"Meaning what, exactly?"

"Meaning that's the way it's done in these circles. Next, you should get a personal visit from

130

the man himself. He'll give you a kiss. I don't know what your set calls that. The Italians call it the kiss of death."

"That's ridiculous," the senator replied, though not too convincingly.

"My sentiments exactly," Bolan said coldly. "But that's still the way it works. And it will be your last happy moment. So savor it. Once the kiss, then swiftly comes the kill." He went on through the doorway and headed for the exit.

Weiss called his name and ran after him. "Let's say you're right!" he cried. "Just for laughs! So tell me, how do you know so much?"

Bolan opened the front door and leaned against the jamb for a final look at the bedeviled man. "Because that's the way I called it," he explained. "I told you I just came from a parley. I laid it out for him. Bonelli wants himself a senator, and he's willing to walk over you buddy's dead body to get one. The solution for Kaufman is simple. He either gives you away or he wastes you. Who's going to fight over a *dead* senator? Figure it, man. It's as simple as one take away one. Who do you think gets the privilege of handpicking your successor in the Senate? Hell. You're expendable."

Bolan went on out and closed the door.

Again the senator pursued, throwing the door open to yell out, "Why do you come telling me this shit? What are you, some kind of a sadist? You come to taunt and walk away?"

Bolan came around with the Beretta in combat crouch. The guy's face went deathly pale and his own weapon sagged toward the ground.

Bolan held the stance as he coldly told the guy with precise enunciation: "You are garbage. I have given thirty minutes of valuable time this day to the salvation of garbage only because many people in this country have no nose for garbage and would therefore mourn your untimely passage. I give no more. What I brought, you take or leave. It makes no difference to me."

That mouth worked briefly before the words came. "But you have it all wrong. I'm no puppet. I run it. Understand me! It's *mine, I* run it!"

Bolan growled, "Run it all the way to hell then."

"Don't shoot! I'm going back inside!"

"Do that," Bolan icily suggested.

The senator who did it all himself did that.

Bolan holstered the Beretta and walked on down the drive. He did not know, yet, how to score the thing—but, for damn sure, *something* had busted loose in Paradise. Only time and the fates would indentify and register the results. But Bolan had not been speaking idly during his closing remarks. He had given all he intended to give. From this point, the devil himself could pick up the marbles.

And maybe the devil wore skirts.

Sharon Kaufman was waiting for him at the curb, a tiny nickle-plated autoloader held knowingly in an unwavering little fist.

"I'm sorry," she said calmly. "Believe me, I am sorry. But I have to do this."

CHAPTER 16

HEARTS

She directed him to a small car parked off the road just uprange from the house and said, "Get behind the wheel. You're driving."

He casually studied the neighborhood for a moment, then followed the direction. If any other hand in Phoenix had been holding that little gun, it would already have been chopped off and its owner left bleeding in the gutter. It could happen yet, but Bolan was giving the girl her moment, letting the thing drift toward a possibly happier conclusion.

She did not even ask for his gun. He did not, of course, offer it. He recognized the car. It had slid into the traffic behind him as he was pulling away from the city hall parley with the girl's father. He had to give her a gold star for the tail job—or perhaps she had simply stumbled onto him at Weiss's place. He wanted to know.

"Congratulations," he said coldly. "You'd make a good detective. I hope you kill as clean as you tail."

"Start the car and drive where I tell you," she said without emotion, ignoring his probe.

He started the car but told her, "No way do I drive where you tell me. I'm returning to my vehicle—and I thank you for the lift. But put the gun away. I don't want to hurt you."

"I'm not kidding," she said calmly. "I'll shoot you if I have to."

"I'd go for the eyes then," he growled.

She did not quite comprehend his meaning.

He put the car in motion as he explained. "Unless you hit a vital spot with the first shot from that peashooter, I'll likely kill you in reflex. So go for the eyes. Put one right through the pupil, angling slightly upward. That should scramble some brain tissue and minimize the reflex action. Of course, there will be a lot of blood and guck ... but I guess you can handle that."

Those young eyes wavered but the voice was steady. "I was on the shooting team at school. And I spent three months on a *kibbutz* in Israel. So don't challenge me. I'm no pushover."

Bolan sighed and sent the car on toward the service area where his battle cruiser awaited. Things were winding down in Arizona . . . and quickly. He really could not afford to spend precious minutes in this fashion. At the same time, the kid had to be dealt with. Obviously there was no talking her down. He pulled in alongside the warwagon and told her, "Fire away."

"I'm making a citizen's arrest. I order you to come peacefully with me to the police station or I *will* shoot."

The girl was twisted about in the seat, facing him, one leg down onto the seat to form a boundary between them, the little pistol resting on the knee in a convincing two-hand hold.

Both of Bolan's big hands came off the steering wheel faster than the girl's eyes could recoil and send the message below—the right smashing backhanded against the side of that pretty face, the left closing over both tiny clutching hands to completely cover them and wrench the little gun from her grasp.

It was no cap pistol. The mighty midget fired in the transfer, booming out with a report much larger than it deserved, punching an expanding slug into the car's dash.

The backhand smash had a shade too much on it, snapping the girl's head back against the doorpost. She was out. The guy with greasy hands from the service station came running over to investigate the disturbance. He instantly recognized Bolan from their earlier encounter, came to a sliding halt, eyes falling to the girl as he exclaimed, "Oh shit! Is she dead?!"

Bolan showed the guy the little nickle-plate as he replied, "She tried to be. Know her?"

The station attendant looked closer, then shook his head. "Never saw her before. What is it? Drugs? Prostitution?"

"Neither," Bolan told him. He got out of the car and went around to the other door, opened it, pulled the girl out. "This is a quiet detail. Understand? So keep it that way. I may need you later for a statement. Meanwhile, cool it."

"Sure, I'll cool it," the guy assured him.

Bolan carried the unconscious girl to the

cruiser and got the hell away from there before the guy could start wondering.

Some minutes and several miles later, the shaken young lady came forward and sagged into the big leather chair at Bolan's side. The cheekbone was slightly swollen and discolored, the eyes a bit glazed, but she seemed generally okay.

"Damn you," she said quietly.

"You almost did," he told her. "Now tell me why."

"I'm an ingrate, huh?" she replied tiredly. "Just because you want to trade my father's life for mine, I should give thanks and wash my hands in his blood. Sorry. It doesn't work that way in this family."

"I hope that's true," he said softly.

He was watching her with about 25 percent of his visual perception. The rest was busy with navigation considerations and vehicular security. The corner of his right eye was surveying a miserable and confused young lady as he told her, "I could have taken your father as easily as I took you on any of three different occasions so far today. But Morris Kaufman lives. So what's all the fuss about?"

"I've seen you operate," she said dispiritedly. "I was at Echo Canyon this morning."

"Yes, I noted your arrival," he told her.

"My father was saved by the grace of God. I simply could not allow you another attempt."

"He was saved by the grace of Bolan," the big man quietly corrected her. "All the attempts on his life have come from downstate. I told you I'd try, Sharon. Dammit, I've been trying."

She was a bit less sure of her position as she

replied to that. "I'd like to believe it. I really would."

"He lives," Bolan simply stated.

The girl drew a shuddering breath and began weeping.

Gruffly, he said, "I'm going to do you a final favor. Truth is sometimes uncomfortable, but you can't build a life of false illusions." He activated the onboard computer and remoted it to the con, then deftly punched in a program code as the warwagon cruised on. Then he angled the viewscreen toward the girl and told her, "This is your life, Morris Kaufman. And the show is sponsored by the United States Department of Justice. I penetrated their computers and taped the entire program."

She peered through wet eyes at the small screen as it lit up with a still photo of her father, blinked rapidly as two others followed in quick succession—right profile, left profile—the sobs choking back as she then settled into an almost trancelike study. The official record of a living cannibal began appearing in electronic display, the speeding lines of dry facts and incredible figures moving almost too fast for the average mind to comprehend. Bolan made an adjustment, slowing the pace for the girl's benefit. Still, it was a dizzying progression of corporate rosters, shady stock transactions, real estate swindles and land grabs, frustrated and hamstrung federal investigations, political clout and governmental corruption, tainted judges and tampered juries—through it all the unmistakable thread of knavery, thievery, mayhem, and murder.

"You're making me sick," she murmured, long before the data bank was exhausted.

Bolan killed the display as he told her, "That's just the tip of the iceberg. Only God and Moe Kaufman know what lies below."

She shuddered, pulled her arms tightly about herself, and turned toward the side window.

Bolan muttered, "Sorry, kid. But you needed it. You'll be facing harder truths . . . and damn soon unless I miss my guess."

"Now I know why mama died," she whispered. "Who could live with that?"

Bolan said nothing, giving the moment to the girl.

Presently she sighed raggedly and said, rather defiantly, "He's still my father. Look at me, dammit."

He looked.

She was unbuttoning her blouse, the fingers trembling and having a bit of trouble with the chore. But the huge breastworks were exposed and jiggling proudly in the release.

Bolan growled, "Cut it out, Sharon."

"Do you find me attractive?"

"I find you entirely appealing. But your timing is lousy."

"Let's make a deal."

He tossed her an unbelieving glance, then slowed the chariot and pulled off the road, crossed his arms over his chest, closed his eyes, and let the chin droop toward the chest.

"Say that again," he muttered.

"Virgin pure . . . almost. Say the word and it's yours."

Without looking up, he growled, "Like father, like daughter. I don't believe this."

"Why not? I'm entirely serious. I'd do anything to . . . stop you."

138

He dug for the little pistol and tossed it to her. "Do what's honest, then," he suggested. "Go ahead and stop me."

Her gaze wavered and fell. She did not pick up the pistol. The tears began flowing again—tears of frustration probably.

More gently, he said, "I've washed my hands of Morris Kaufman. He's the author of his own fate—and probably nothing I could do would rewrite that script now. Loyalty is a great thing, Sharon, when loyalty has been earned. But it's a lousy kick in the cosmic seat when blind loyalty supersedes everything noble and good in the human experience. It's time you face that."

But she was not yet ready to face it. The blouse was completely off now. She cupped the breasts in both hands and urged those delicacies toward him. "I'll go with you wherever you say. For however long you say. Just save him. Please. Save him for *me*."

"Get off it!" he growled with false anger. "It's time you learned what *I* am all about. You think my work is so casual that my decisions come from my loins? Think again, kid. And cover yourself up. I'm not all that damn immune to invited rape."

"You'd rape my heart, though, without a thought. Yes, I know what you're all about, Mack Bolan. You have a grim reaper complex."

"Call it any way that comforts you," he replied coldly. He put the vehicle in motion. "And get dressed. I'm dropping you at the first opportunity."

But, yeah, his heart hurt for her.

It always hurt for such as these, the innocent victims of jungle justice.

But Mack Bolan's combat decisions came not from the heart, either. They came from the injured seat of a kicked cosmos. The Executioner was simply kicking back.

CHAPTER 17

RIFT

Yeah, the Arizona game was winding down quickly, for sure. Bolan's intelligence computer was fairly running over with collections from the automated monitoring stations—and the big problem of the past twenty minutes had been to simply sort and assimilate the fast pace of events.

Weiss and Kaufman provided a say-nothing shouting match via telephone, followed by a promised eyeball meet at Weiss's home "damn quick!"

Paul Bonelli, "heir" to Arizona, and his forty fighting guns from Tucson had gone to ground near an old airstrip in the desert, waiting only for the night to cloak their "mop-up" movements.

Hinshaw and company were maintaining the diggings at their own base camp, bolstered now by a thirty-man "reserve force" of fully equipped combat troops—also awaiting nightfall.

Old man Nick Bonelli was flapping his wings and threatening to fly to Phoenix to take the entire operation under his personal command.

There was obvious bad blood developing between Hinshaw and the younger Bonelli—and it sounded as though the old man was actively promoting some sort of iron-handed show of strength by his kid. Interesting as hell though, was the obvious fact that neither Bonelli knew of Hinshaw's secret reserves.

Bolan chewed that for several minutes, trying to pull Hinshaw's motives into focus and trying also to come up with a quick but viable play to exploit that possibility of rift in the opposing forces.

He finally opted for a frontal approach, spinning back to a telephone contact wherein the phone number of Paul's encampment was recorded. Then he called that number from the warwagon's mobile equipment and told the answering voice, "It's urgent. Get Mr. Bonelli."

A moment later, he had the heir to Arizona on the horn. "The name is Lambretta. I'm connected . . . east. You may remember a guy, Billy Gino."

"Yeah?"

"Billy's my cousin. I came down from Vegas a few days back."

"So?"

"I owe, uh, I owe Don Bonelli an old favor. You may not remember . . . the South Bronx rumble back in, uh . . . ."

"I r'member, sure. What'd you say your name was?"

"I'm using Lambretta right now, Mr. Bonelli. You, uh, understand. Listen, what I got is this. I just came from a joint on the east side, a very

142

weird joint, Mr. Bonelli. Out in the damn sand, you know. Looks like it got blasted pretty bad, and not long ago. There's a guy there calls himself Morales—a greaser, acting like a head cock. Does any of this sound like anything you know?"

"Maybe and maybe not," Bonelli replied cautiously. "What are you getting to, Lambretta? Let's get there."

"This Morales tried to recruit me. He wouldn't say for what, but he dropped your name. He offered me five thou for a night's work."

"What the hell!" Bonelli growled angrily. "You call me urgent to confirm a lousy job offer?"

"No sir, that's not why I called. Like I said, I owe Don Bonelli. The greaser don't know I'm calling you."

The guy's reply to that was mixed with irritation and open curiosity. "How the hell did you get this number then?"

"Hey! Mr. Bonelli! I been connected a long time. You don't need to ask a soldier of the blood how he—"

"Okay, okay! What've you got?"

"Something very cutesy about that joint, sir. The guy has a damn combat force out there . . . must be forty or fifty boys with heavy heat. Not a damn one is a made man . . . no connections there anywhere. He says—"

"Wait a minute, wait! How many you say? *Forty* or *fifty*!? How long ago was this?"

"Not an hour ago. What I was gonna say . . . nobody connected, except he wants *me* out front. He says for identification. He says so Mr. Bonelli will know it's the right place. It stinks, don't it? It stinks to me."

"Maybe it does, yeah," Bonelli replied, the tone
143

thoughtful. "How'd you say you come to get out there?"

"This Morales came looking for a connected man. He found me through a, uh, mutual friend."

"He's pretty damn stupid then, isn't he?" said the heir. "He doesn't understand the blood, does he? You say forty or fifty boys under arms out there? How'd you happen to get loose?"

"I told him, sure, I'd take the job. But I had some business in town first. I'm supposed to be back by sundown."

"Don't go back," Bonelli said softly.

"Don't worry."

"If this checks out, you look us up in Tucson some day. If it don't, well . . ."

"I gave you what I got, sir. Exactly."

"He says you're up front for indentification, eh?"

"Yessir. The idiot. Any man with connections knows what that means. Right?"

"Right, right. Thanks, uh, Lambretta. You look us up in Tucson. We'll show you the town."

Bolan hung it up and made an imaginary mark in the air above his head, then immediately called the other force.

Hinshaw himself answered the ring, indentifying with a curt, "Hinshaw. What?"

"This is Bolan."

A brief silence, then: "Well hello. How'd you find me?"

"You were easy," Bolan said pleasantly.

"When did you tumble it was me?"

"I caught a glimpse of Worthy and Morales. Put it together. What are you trying to do to me, soldier?"

The guy chuckled. "I might ask the same of you."

"You're screwing me up," Bolan said, the tone still entirely pleasant.

"I guess that's the idea. Beans are beans, you know. Makes no difference who cooks them or serves them."

"So how much is he paying you?"

"You want to make a counteroffer?"

"Right."

"I'm getting 200 a day plus."

"Plus what?"

"All I can steal," Hinshaw replied laughing. "What are you prepared to offer?"

"Guess I can't top that," Bolan said. "Not the plus, anyway. Forget it. All I can offer is about twelve hours."

They were getting down to business, and Hinshaw's tone reflected an understanding of that fact. "Twelve hours of what?"

"Life," Bolan said quietly.

"Come on."

"Seriously. And I can't guarantee even that much. It all depends on Paul."

It was a forced laugh that came across that connection. "Good try, soldier. Whatever you're trying."

"Any victory for them is a loss for me," Bolan said soberly. "I'd throw in with the devil if they were storming hell."

The guy's interest was aroused, despite the natural caution. "I'll listen. Say what you're saying."

"I have the whole state wired. I even have you wired, soldier. And I challenge you to find the—"

Hinshaw broke in to unload a disturbance of

145

his own mind. "Yeah, tell me about that, pole climber. How'd you engineer that hit?"

"You found the hardware."

"Sure. And what about Tucson?"

"I was there," Bolan admitted.

"What kind of explosives did you hit me with? Angel swears you were under surveillance the whole time. What'd you use?"

It was shop talk between a couple of professionals. Bolan replied, "Something I whipped up in my lab. Time delayed. How'd it go?"

"Just like Ex-Lax, smooth as silk. Did you design that box for the fifty?"

"Something else I cooked up in my lab, yeah. She didn't jam up, eh?"

"Not hardly. It's a beautiful effect. I'm taking it with me when I break camp here. It'll come in handy somewhere, some day. You wired me, too, huh? We searched, man. Where is it?"

"About two miles downline. Climb a pole where the barrel cactus stands. You'll find it. Keep it, it's a gift—to remember me by. If you're able to remember."

"You were saying? About wires on the state?"

"Yeah. I have very sophisticated stuff. You'd love it. Straight out of the space age. Hear-all, know-all—you know what I mean. They're setting you up, soldier. I could have guessed it, even without the ears. It's SOP with these people. Contract a dirty job, see. That's a security layer. Then contract the contractor. That's another layer. The point is, it was never intended that you get the chance to enjoy that 200 per day plus."

The returning voice was sober, wary. "You're giving me this just for old-time's sake, eh?"

"The past is the past," Bolan said. "You did

146

your thing and I did mine. Anyway, it was long ago and far away. This is here and now. Far as I'm concerned, you are a fellow grunt getting another shaft. Take it or don't, makes no difference to me. But I hate to see those bastards get away with it."

"You'd hate that, eh?"

"I'd hate it, yeah. Watch your flanks, soldier."

Bolan put the phone down and made another imaginary mark in the air, then changed his mind and erased half of it.

The game was winding down, yeah. And Bolan was down for doubles.

CHAPTER 18

PAWNS OUT

Abraham Weiss loved the sunlight. Others may take comfort in the moderate Arizona winters, but Weiss preferred the burning heat of summer because it also meant more hours of daylight in each twenty-four.

Not that he was *afraid* of the *dark*.

He would not admit that even to himself. He just preferred the sunlight. One reason he hated Washington was the damn short days—especially in winter. God, how he hated Washington in the winter!

But he definitely had mixed feelings about these desert sunsets. So beautiful to behold, sure, but sort of like dying, also. Even *knowing* that the sun also rises, there was something very sad and tragic in a sunset.

Like a man's life, slowly waning, waning, waning . . . then *snuff!*—gone—blackness—nothingness.

He shivered and stepped away from the window. Another hour of daylight. So where the hell was Moe! And where the hell was all this police protection he'd been promised! Leave a man hanging out here like the final damn grape on the vine, just waiting for someone to come along and *snuff*!

That kind of thinking would get him nowhere!

He crossed to the desk, opened the secret panel, reversed the tape on the recorder, and played back that ridiculous telephone conversation with his lifelong *buddy*, Moe Kaufman.

Some buddy.

"Goddammit, Abe, sometimes I think you're getting senile! You can't pay any attention to a guy like that! He's just trying to get us scratching at each other's eyes."

"Did he talk to you or didn't he?"

"Yes, dammit, he talked to me. Walked right into the police station, and we sat in an empty office and talked for about five minutes."

"Go get fucked, you miserable . . . I'm not *that* senile! Why are you holding out on me?"

"Listen, I'm coming out there. Personally, I'm bringing you some new comfort. Now just sit tight and wait till I get there."

"I can pick up this phone and place one call . . . *one* call. I could call Cronkite. Hell, I could call the White House if I wanted to. If you're playing cute games with me . . . ."

"For God's sake, Abe. Get ahold. Can't you see what you're doing?"

"It will be getting dark soon, Moe. I don't want to be here alone when it gets dark."

149

"Buck up. I'm on my way."

"Come alone!"

"Are you crazy? Why should I come alone? I'm bringing *comfort*, dammit!"

"I won't be here, Moe. I swear. I'm leaving."

"Don't you *dare* leave that house! It's the only protection you've got for now. Do you want me to send a police car screaming to the rescue? Is that what you want?"

"I don't know. Maybe so. Yeah. I want them in uniform. I want a whole goddamn platoon of uniformed cops."

"You know better. We're trying to quiet this, not put it on the evening news. We can't afford that kind of—"

"*We* can't afford it?! That's rich, that's really rich."

"Put a gun in your hand, dammit, and sit tight. I'll be there."

Sure. He'd be here. When? In time for the second coming? The Senator stared at the desk clock. Was it stopped? Could a clock move that slowly and still be working properly?

Ridiculous! Such a ridiculous and demeaning conversation! *That* tape should be destroyed. Who'd want something like *that* in the memoirs?

Ridiculous, absolutely. Moe was right. Bolan was just trying to confuse things, sow dissension.

That clock could not be working. How long had it been? Why wasn't he *here*?

He toyed with the Browning, checked the clip, tested the action, removed the clip and ejected the round from the magazine, put it back in the clip, returned the clip . . . oh, God *dammit*!

A man should not be alone at a time like this. A

man should have friends, family, someone who cared. . . .

Moe Kaufman was the only true friend he'd ever had. True? True to what? True to Abraham Weiss? Hell no, not so. Moe Kaufman did not befriend. Moe Kaufman merely *used*.

A puppet, huh? That son of a bitch! Where'd he get off calling Abraham Weiss a *puppet*? Pawn, maybe. Yeah. Pawn.

What was that?

Had he heard something? Carlos?

Of course not. They'd sent Carlos away hours ago.

But someone was in the house!

Expendable, huh! Abraham Weiss was *expendable*! He snatched up the Browning and whirled to the door, screaming, *"Bullshit! Bullshit!"*

A dark form materialized in the gloom of that doorway, something glinting from an outstretched hand. And then the two persons who lived inside the body of Abraham Weiss parted, separated into two, fragmenting that consciousness. The one quickly raised the Browning and sighted coolly into the squeeze; the other stood back in horror, stunned by the thunderous report of the bucking pistol. Something grunted and pitched forward into the room, while something else moved in quickly to take its place, making startled sounds and calling out in alarm. Part One squeezed the trigger again and then again, as Part Two awoke with dismay as Old Friend Moe screamed at him from the doorway—but too late came the awakening. Part One was still squeezing, squeezing, squeezing—and the Browning roared on until there was nothing but dull clicks to be heard from the automatic movements of that trigger finger.

Something clicked, also, inside Abe Weiss's head.

The Browning fell to the floor and he sank into his chair, hands clasped across the belly, bent forward, eyes straining into the gloom.

"Moe? Is that you? Moe?"

He turned on the desk lamp and looked again.

Two men lay crumpled on the floor just inside the room. He hesitantly got to his feet and went over for a cautious closer look. God, he'd drilled them perfect. God, they were dead as hell. Take that, dammit. Issue paper on Abe Weiss, will you. Fuck you.

He stepped over the corpses and ventured into the hall, finding the light switch, illuminating a scene straight from hell.

Old Friend Moe lay on his back in a pool of blood, dead eyes staring up at Old Friend Abe and mirroring shock—surprise—what? Take that, Old Friend Moe. Take that, you fucking pawn. Expendable, huh?

Self-defense. Clearly it was self-defense. They'd come to get him, to expend him, to replace him with virgin flesh untainted by the competitions of a corrupt world. Fuck them all. It was self-defense, pure and simple.

He returned to the den where all his trophies of the hunt now shared honors with the trophies of survival.

They'd come in with guns drawn—he knew that for sure—he'd seen the glint of gunmetal lifting into the pull.

Abraham Weiss? Are you Senator Abraham Weiss?

Sure. Identify yourself so they know they got the right cookie. There's no profit in gunning the wrong cookie.

He turned one of them with a foot and knelt for a closer inspection of that gunmetal.

Shit. Oh shit.

Self-defense. It was self-defense!

Against a badge, Abe? The man came in with a badge in his hand and you gunned him down?

Cop killer!

You fucking lunatic! You killed two cops and your best friend—*you killed your comfort!*

He went back to the desk and sat down. The sun would be setting soon.

Yeah. Yeah. The sun would be setting very soon, now, for Honest Abe Weiss.

CHAPTER 19

SCORE

Bolan was hoping to engineer a climactic shootout at the OK corral. And why not? It was the Wild West, wasn't it? The combined force would number perhaps a hundred guns. Those were odds that were best avoided whenever possible. Bolan very much desired to avoid them. If he could persuade them to decimate themselves, though . . .

He swung past the Hinshaw encampment at a cautious distance and triggered a final data collection. Even if Hinshaw had bought the tip-off on the wires, it was still possible that there had not been time yet for him to locate and disable the little black box.

The intelligence console was sucking something in. Bolan gave it time to assimilate the intel while he continued the wary circling of the enemy camp. He struck off cross-country, the big cruiser running easily on the desert surface, running up their back side at about a thousand yards out.

Then the computer flashed him a signal. He sent the necessary response and activated the audio monitor.

And it was a real score.

The senior Bonelli, all triumphant and gloating, was on the horn with Jim Hinshaw.

"Did Paul get there yet?"

"Sir, I need to tell you right off to be careful. We think there may be other ears on this line."

"Whose are they?"

"We think maybe Bolan."

The *Capo Arizona* scoffed at that. "Let 'im listen. It's all over, Jimmy. It's bagged. Put Paul on."

"We don't expect him till sundown, sir."

That didn't sit well. "I guess he's betwixt and between, then. I couldn't raise him at the other joint. Listen. I'm coming up there. They're rolling the plane out right now. You know where we'll land."

"Yes, sir."

"Pass this to Paul soon as he gets there. Pass this. It's bagged. The golden opportunity is meeting me at the airfield. I want Paul there, too. We're going south for awhile. Not Guatemala but the other—he'll understand."

"Pardon me, sir, but—"

"I'm not finished. You're still passing, now. Paul is to hot it over to the golden opportunity's joint and go right in. Don't be surprised at what he finds there. He'll understand it all, then. And he's to clean up that garbage. That's the important part, Jimmy. Clean up the garbage. I want it spotless. You get all that?"

"Yes, sir, I got it all," Hinshaw replied feebly. "Where does this leave me?"

"Sitting pretty," Bonelli said jovially. "There'll be bonuses all around. Take it on back down to the home digs and wait till you hear from me."

"I don't, uh, think I understand, sir. What about Bolan?"

"What about 'im?"

"Well, uh . . . the guy is still blasting around. Does *he* know it's all bagged?"

Bonelli laughed nastily. "Let's tell 'im. Hey, Bolan. You there? Been laid lately? No? Here's my advice to you, then. Go get fucked."

"Mr.—sir, I don't think—I mean, shit, pardon me but *nothing* is bagged. This whole damn town is crackling with that guy."

The *capo* was not to be deflated. "Let 'im crackle. We got what we wanted. Get it down, now, Jimmy, and dare the guy to come in. The feds are pouring into the state from every direction. They're even sending Border Patrol after the guy. Just get it down and wait 'im out. He'll be moving on at first dark. I'll bet my life on that."

"Can I speak plain, sir?"

"You might as well."

"What about Scorecard?"

"What the hell you think I been telling you? It's bagged."

"You mean . . . ?"

"That's what I mean. That's the garbage. How plain can I say it?"

"But how—what—I mean . . ."

Bonelli cackled over the spluttering Hinshaw's discomfort. "Golden opportunity did it for us," he howled.

"Well I'll be damned," Hinshaw marveled.

156

"Yeah. Rich, huh? He came over. On his own. So . . . see? You were doing more up there than you thought you were."

"He fragged 'im!" Hinshaw roared.

"Yeah, goddammit, ain't that rich?"

"I'll pass it to Paul, sir. I can hardly wait."

"The cleanup is important. Be sure and pass that. We don't want golden opportunity facing no rap like that."

"Oh, hey, right. I see what you mean."

"The plane's ready, Jimmy. Listen. Here's what I want *you* to do. Bring your boys out to the field. Just in case."

"We'll cover it, sir. Don't worry. You'll have a clean field."

"Yeah. See to that."

End of recording.

Bolan punched the timer code and frowned at the response. The conversation had been recorded about ten minutes earlier. And he understood the significance of that guarded conversation. Obviously Weiss and Kaufman had dissolved their partnership. Now Kaufman lay dead in the senator's home and Weiss had gone to Bonelli for help.

Scorecard, eh?

If Bolan were to code-name his own operation, now, he would have to call it *Backfire*. He'd leaned on the Kosher Nostra for specific effect, sure—but not for this one.

It was the *one* possible result never visualized.

Backfire, yeah.

But maybe it was not too late to pull it out. The Hinshaw compound now lay just over the ridge. The sun had not yet set. Bonelli's "plane" could hardly be more than barely off the ground at Tucson.

So. It was not bagged yet. *Are you listening, Nick? Have you been laid lately? Yes? Take this advice from me, then. Too much score can make the brain go soft.*

Stay hard, Nick.

Stay as hard as you can because it's not bagged yet.

The cute was ended. Only the hellfire remained.

CHAPTER 20

FRAGGED

Hinshaw stepped from the doorway of the command hut and raised a finger to summon his executive officer. Morales drifted over, a cigarette dangling from parched lips.

"Make sure the grunts are set and ready," Hinshaw told him. "Something's out of whack here. Way out."

"Maybe our old buddy was leveling with us."

Hinshaw worriedly shook his head. "Nothing figures. That's what makes it so damn scary. I'll say one thing for Bolan. He knows these guys like a fisherman knows worms. I don't trust them as far as I can fart."

"It's the devil or the deep blue," Morales agreed. "I'll say this. If I gotta face Bolan or them, I'd settle for them."

"We may be facing *both*," Hinshaw groused. "I just had a crazy talk with the old man. He says it's over. He says we achieved all the objectives. Can you buy that?"

Morales spat. "Shit," he said.

"He says Weiss fragged Kaufman and came over. How does that sound?"

Morales rethought it. "Maybe. That's what I'd do. If I had Mack fucking Bolan *and* the whole bloody Mafia on my ass. Yeah. I'd frag the Jew."

"So maybe it does figure," Hinshaw mused.

"But you're still worried."

"I'm worried, Angel, yeah."

"Okay. I'll make a round and set the men. Can I make a suggestion?"

"If it's not too long."

"Don't tip our hand to Paul Bonelli. Keep him outside. Let's keep the card in the hole."

"I was thinking the same thing. But it may be easier said than done. I had it all figured till the old man slipped me a klinker. I don't know how to figure it now. But you're right. We keep Junior outside. If the old man is setting us up . . . . But why would he do that now? Either he's leveling—which sounds sort of crazy—or he's setting us up before the job is even done—and that's even crazier. Set the men. I'm going down to the gate. I got a message for Junior. We'll play it their way and see what happens. But carefully, Angel—very carefully."

Morales winked and walked away. Hinshaw lit a cigarette and gazed at the horizon. He hoped that blood-red sky was not portentous. James Ray Hinshaw fervently desired to spend every cent of that 200 plus per day . . . especially the *plus*. The *plus,* especially.

Paul Bonelli halted his motorcade at the rendezvous point and leaned out the window to greet his forward scout.

"What'd you find?" he asked the guy.

"They've set up a couple of big tents and moved most of their goods inside them. Looks like they cleaned up and made a bonfire out of those damaged buildings. There's only a couple of shacks still standing."

"How many people?"

"Not many I could see. Here and there, a guy standing or sitting. The Morales kid keeps walking around very restless."

Bonelli grunted as he tried to digest that. "How many cars?" he asked.

"Just what they had before. But a lot of brush has been piled in the canyon out back. They could have a Hertz fleet back in there somewhere."

"Give me your bone feel, Ernie."

The scout shrugged. "It looks okay. But I got creepy just lookin' at it."

"Did you scout the hills?"

"Best I could with the time I had. A camper rolled through a few minutes ago, heading north. That's all."

"What kind of camper?"

"One of those big RVs. GMC, I think. Looked clean."

Bonelli sighed. "Hell. I don't know any more than I did before. Why would the guy call me with a story like that?"

"You know how some wise guys are, boss. Anything for a quick mark or a free meal. He hopes you'll remember it as a kind thought that was just a little wrong."

"It stinks," Bonelli snapped. "How good could you see into that joint? If he was trying to hide something in there, could you have tumbled to it?"

"That's hard to say, boss. But you can always hide what you don't want seen."

"And it creeped you."

"Right. It creeped me."

"That's good enough for me. Send the crew bosses up here. We'll parley. Then we'll move in."

"Are we moving hard?"

"Bet your ass we're moving hard," Bonelli assured the scout.

Damn right. The soldier boy was not going to frag *this* C.O. The brotherhood of the blood, by Jesus, had *invented* that little game. Paul Bonelli had been *born* to it.

Sure as hell he was not going to die by it.

Bolan took the ridge in a grimly silent struggle, a garrote buried deeply in sentry flesh. Then he dragged the guy to the back side and returned to the battle cruiser for the strike weapons—selecting the Weatherby sniper, an M-79, and two belts of 40mm rounds in mixed configuration.

Back at the ridge again—the same one from which the earlier cutesy strike had been launched—he spurned the drop chosen by the dead sentry and moved on down to an outcropping of rock situated just above the camp.

It was optimum range for the M-79 hellraiser and the overlook gave him a full 90-degree sweep into the flatlands.

He laid out the belts and thumbed in a round of high explosive for openers, then placed the wicked little launcher aside and raised the glasses for a quick recon of the combat zone.

A procession of heavy vehicles broke the horizon, moving swiftly, closing—one, two, hell, eight big crew wagons.

Directly below, the Hinshaw camp was coming alive—guys scurrying about in desert denims, blending far too well with that arid landscape— getting set for a blow.

Bolan smiled grimly as he picked up the Weatherby.

Yeah. It was likely to be a hell of a blow.

They came roaring in like a wild horse stampede, raising a cloud of dust that trailed out for a half a mile behind, single-filing it until the last fifty yards or so, then wheeling it over in a fancy maneuver that put all eight cars in rank abreast, nose to the fence.

Hinshaw growled, "Lookit that. What the hell is he doing?"

Bonelli cracked a window to call over, "Send your boys out, Jimmy. We'll use our wheels. We got plenty of room."

Hinshaw flipped away his cigarette, gripped the gate with both hands, and called back, "It's all changed. Word from your papa. Come on in."

The only immediate response to that was an abrupt raising of Bonelli's window. Hinshaw stood woodenly at the gate, wondering what the hell, feeling like a fool.

Long seconds elapsed.

A door opened and a guy stepped out—one of the crew bosses, a Tucson hotshot. "Mr. Bonelli wants you to come talk to him," hotshot announced.

"What the hell is this?" Hinshaw yelled. "You tell Mr. Bonelli I'm here, looking at him. I got a message from his papa. But I sure as hell ain't going along with *this* shit!"

The window came back down. Bonelli stuck his head out cautiously. "What's the message?"

"What the hell are you *doing?*" Hinshaw cried. "What am I suddenly, a leper? I don't talk to you this way, Paul."

"What's the message?"

Hinshaw ground his teeth together. It was true then. Bolan had it pegged for sure. He was about to fling an angry retort at the traitorous bastard when something quite remarkable got there first.

Paul Bonelli's face simply disintegrated. The mouth turned dark and gaping, the nose collapsed into it, the eyes disappeared and the whole miserable mess disintegrated into frothy pulp. The wheelman yelled something and lunged away from those spraying juices. Only then did the sound overtake the macabre scene, a hollow boom from somewhere up the canyon, and it was James Hinshaw's turn to react. He flung himself into the dust and rolled like crazy for the closest cover, a shallow depression near the gatepost, his mind racing ahead into the numbing understanding of what would immediately, inevitably, follow.

The hotshot crew boss was the next to go spinning off into eternity, caught dead in his tracks as he sprinted for the protected side of his vehicle, down and wallowing in deflated flesh even before the second big boom came down.

And then it was 'Nam all over again, ambush in the wilderness, a hundred frenzied weapons in reflexive fire as hell came down all around—and Jim Hinshaw flat in the middle.

Several of the crew wagons from Tucson lurched forward, punching through the flimsy fence in angry retort, muzzles blazing from every window.

Jim Hinshaw knew that it was all a horrible mistake.

But he was obviously the only one there who knew it. The guy with the big boomer knew it. Yeah, Bolan knew it.

And Jim Hinshaw knew, in a highly personal sense, what it was like to be the fraggee. He'd been had ... by an expert.

And that went double for Bonelli Junior.

CHAPTER 21

BAGGED

Bolan had monitored through binoculars the tense confrontation at the compound gate, read it accurately, sealed it with a thundering kiss from the Weatherby—then played the reaction entirely by ear.

The Bonelli force read the attack as treachery from the Hinshaw camp. Morales, commanding at the rear and unable to precisely understand the unfolding events, held no options whatever in the face of the furious retaliatory attack by the Bonelli guns. The inevitable result was a blazing firefight between two "friendly" forces.

And Bolan assisted that development, also, with a few touches from the background. He raised the '79, sighted down on an invading hardwagon just inside the compound, and sent them some HE. The big vehicle heeled immediately and wallowed to a halt in enveloping flames. A following round of smoke deposited at the gate further confused the landscape there—then a rapid shoestring of alternating HE and Frag laced that hellground with walking destruction and cascading pandemonium.

The staccato chatter of automatic weapons mingled with the echoing booms of busy shotguns and the angry yapping of pistols as the clash of arms quickly reached full fury.

Hinshaw's "reserves" were no pantywaist platoon. It was a disciplined and combat-worthy fireteam—equal to anything Bolan had seen in 'Nam. Except for the Bolan influence, there would have been no doubt as to the outcome of that battle. Those guys knew what they were about—and they had the heavy arms to back up the expertise. A heavy machine gun was chewing ass all along the Bonelli front until Bolan spotted it and took it out. Likewise another couple of well-emplaced units with grenade launchers which were playing havoc with the streetcorner cowboys from Tucson.

Within forty seconds after the fight erupted, all five penetrating Bonelli "tanks" were destroyed and burning. The entire area was strewn with the dead and dying from both sides. Cautious movements in both directions signaled the approaching lull and probable stalemate. Neither side had much fight left. Bolan could count a mere handful of survivors in desert denims, about the same for the other side. Smoke and dust clouded the tableau, restricting visibility and aiding the cautious withdrawal of both sides.

The three Bonelli vehicles which had remained beyond the fence line were now maneuvering carefully to pick up retreating survivors.

Bolan caught a flash glimpse of another vehicle

within the compound—Angel Morales, he thought, at the wheel—also maneuvering carefully to shield a sprinting ghost from the past, the one and only James Ray Hinshaw.

Bolan was gathering his weapons and preparing to quit that place when the Bonelli vehicles sped away into the sunset. A moment later, two cars emerged from the rear area of the compound and raced off in obvious pursuit.

Bolan grinned soberly and returned to his cruiser.

He set the navigation gear for automatic track and began the final maneuver, he hoped, of the battle for Arizona.

Weiss stood in the shadow of a delapidated hangar and watched a sleek twin-engine Cessna jet as it taxied out of the hated sunset and braked to a halt.

Two burly gorillas immediately descended to the ground, nostrils flaring warily as they separated and energetically strode to flanking defensive positions beside the plane. Weiss knew that he would have to become accustomed to such unsavory presences in his life; he would be seeing a lot of it from this point forward.

A moment later, the *Capo Arizona* himself appeared in the doorway and made a quick exit.

The senator experienced an involuntary tremor as he stepped forward to grasp that entrapping hand. They were not exactly strangers, of course. But overt contacts with the likes of Nick Bonelli were not apt to produce the most desirable public image for an elected official. There had been no social relationship whatever.

One would think that nothing whatever had happened.

The *mafioso* gave him a sober smile and greeted him with, "Hi, Senator. Long time no see."

Weiss could not return the smile. "I appreciate this, Nick," he said solemnly.

The guy made a funny little twitch with his lips as he replied, "What are friends for?"

"Did you take care of it?" Weiss inquired nervously.

"Before I left home, yeah. Forget it. It never happened. When my boys get done with it, you'll have a hard time believing what happened yourself."

"I don't want to know the details."

"Who's giving any? The less said the better."

They went into a little office beside the hangar. Bonelli guided him to a dusty chair, offered him a cigar, went to the window and craned his neck to scrutinize the approaches, mumbled something to himself, went to a scarred desk and perched atop it.

"What are we waiting for?" Weiss asked irritably.

"My boy Paul is coming with us. You ever been to Costa Rica?"

Weiss shook his head, smiling sourly. "We get few junkets in that direction. I called my Washington office right after I talked to you. Told them I'd be out of the country for a few days."

"That's fine," Bonelli replied. "Be a bit longer than that, though. A few little details left to be cleaned up around here. It don't need us. We'll get some sun. Play some golf. You play golf?"

"Every chance I get," Weiss said, warming a bit to this strange mixture of thug and charmer.

"I seal more deals on the golf course than . . ."

Bonelli's eyes flashed to the window.

A car was approaching.

The *Capo Arizona* slid off the desk and said, "Here's Paul. Let's go."

It was *three* cars—moving fast and burning rubber as they braked to swing off the blacktop road.

Hell, they looked . . . . They were! All shot up! Shattered window glass!

Bonelli growled, "Holy . . . !"

The two torpedoes at the plane spun away and raced to place themselves between the don and the approaching vehicles.

"It's okay!" Bonelli yelled to them. "They're ours!"

Weiss started off nervously toward the plane, halting about halfway to peer back at the unfolding drama.

The cars were lurching to a halt near the office.

Bonelli, swaying anxiously beside the leading car, speaking animatedly to someone inside. Bonelli, jerking the front door open and nearly ripping off the hinges. Bonelli, head thrown back in a soundless scream, pounding on the roof of that broken car with a jackhammer fist. Bonelli, leaning inside to drag out a human form—a terribly limp and obviously broken human form. Bonelli, tearfully clutching a horribly mutilated and soggy-looking once-human head to his breast. Bonelli, bearing up a dead son and staggering with his burden toward the plane.

All it really meant to Abraham Weiss was that something had gone terribly sour.

"Did they take care of it?" he gasped as the *Capo Arizona* staggered past with his gruesome burden.

"Let's go!" Bonelli croaked in passing. "Get inna plane!"

Other vehicles were approaching.

Energetic men were spilling from the parked cars and scurrying frantically toward defensible positions.

Weiss came unglued and ran on to the Cessna to shrinkingly assist with the boarding of Paul Bonelli's pitiful remains. The bodyguards roughly shoved the senator inside and hastily secured the door.

And it had. Yes, obviously. It had all gone terribly sour. And now the sun was also down—perhaps never to rise again for Abraham Weiss.

The Hinshaw raiders were keeping the Tucson survivors well occupied in the hangar area, the rippling explosions of an erupting firefight signaling an end to the chase.

Bolan had no further interest whatever in that chase—nor in the participants. Both had served his purpose.

He left the cruiser parked beside the blacktop road and set off cross-country on foot, hurrying toward the south end of the runway with the M-79—sampling the wind and reading the aerodynamic considerations, thinking like the pilot of an aircraft. He knew the guy would make his takeoff roll to the south, into the wind.

Someone else apparently had the same idea.

A battered car was jouncing along the uneven surface of the desert floor, making a wide circle to avoid the conflict of arms at the hangar—on a course to directly intercept Bolan's.

And they'd spotted him. At about sixty yards out, the vehicle veered to home directly on the running figure, pistol fire blazing at him from the window on the passenger side.

He flung himself to the prone without breaking stride, rolling and twisting upon impact to squeeze off a do-or-die round from the '79.

The HE round dug sand at the front bumper of the charging car, the hurried and off-balance shot scoring a near-miss, which nevertheless gutted the engine compartment from below, and diverting the charge.

The car quivered, heeled, and took a roll toward the runway.

The M-79 had taken a load of sand in the breech. Unable to immediately free the action, Bolan tossed the weapon aside and pursued the stricken vehicle with a big silver pistol, the .44 Automag, up and ready.

Two men were in that vehicle—Morales and Hinshaw—Angel at the wheel, James Ray "riding shotgun."

They'd rode her through two full rolls to a shuddering upright position. Morales was unconscious, the head dangling off to the shoulder at a crazy angle. Hinshaw's right arm hung loosely, also at an odd angle, from the window. It had been caught outside in the roll and was now bleeding profusely, obviously broken.

The guy gave him a sick smile at he groaned, "Guess it's just you'n me now, stud."

"Wrong," Bolan said coldly. "It's just you and you."

He walked on past, gained the runway, and

turned north. The firefight was sputtering to a close. Of more importance, a twin-engine Cessna was winding up screaming jets and launching itself into high roll, departing that combat zone with all possible haste.

Bolan moved to the center of the runway and jogged on. 100 yards . . . 90 . . . 80—no man's land was shrinking fast as the screaming jet bore down on him. At fifty yards he dropped to one knee, coolly sighted the big pistol, and went into rapid unload.

All eight rounds went home, but none, apparently, found a vital spot. He ejected and clicked in a fresh load with the plane practically on top of him, the wheels now lifting into the take-off.

There was one of those stop-action moments—a mere microsecond of eternal time which somehow expands to fill all of eternity—in which he was eyeball to eyeball with Honest Abe Weiss. As viewed through the eye, the Senator was just beyond the windshield of that hurtling craft, that timeworn face contorted in a grimace of horror; as viewed through the trapdoor of expanded time and space, he was standing outside his home in Paradise, a Browning skullbuster dangling ineffectively in trembling grasp, declaring for the wide world to hear: "I run it. It's mine, I run it!"

"Run it all the way to hell then," Bolan had told him.

He told him now, in para-time, "You ran it too hard, Abe."

And then the lifting plane was flashing up and over him, he was toppling onto his back and taking cool measurements, again stroking the fire of that spectacular .44.

They went home that time—all of them, each of them.

The sleek jet staggered. Flames whoofed along the wing. She tried to go straight up then seemed to halt dead in the air momentarily at a couple hundred feet up—but that was an optical illusion produced by over-the-horizon reds from the setting sun clashing with over-the-wing flames from a setting plane.

She blew straight up—and the flare from that explosion was probably seen in Paradise.

But the scattered and settling fragments would perhaps never be seen again—except maybe a glimpse now and then in some corner of expanded time and space.

The Executioner sheathed his weapon and muttered, "Bag that, Nick." Then he quickly put that place behind him.

And it was okay.

This time, father cosmos had picked up all the marbles.

EPILOGUE

Other hellgrounds beckoned. He knew they always would so long as he lived.

But there were those times, those moments, when Eden deserved a bit of attention also.

So it was no misdirection of the mind that sent the world's most wanted fugitive back along the cosmic curve to a winding drive in Paradise.

The odds were, of course, that she would just give him another kick in the seat of the pants and sent him on to the next blood river.

But a corner of the Bolan mind held a lot of hope for Morris Kaufman's kid.

At the very least, she deserved to be told of her father's death by someone who cared. Bolan cared.

So maybe they could find some basis for mutual understanding. It was the least he could offer.

And maybe, despite all that separated them, they

could pull together the fragmented corners of a brief respite in Paradise.

What the hell.

Mother Cosmos deserved equal time . . . didn't she?

A SELECTED LIST OF
CRIME STORIES
PUBLISHED BY CORGI

☐	10682 8	THE WARY TRANSGRESSOR	*James Hadley Chase* 60p
☐	10681 X	SO WHAT HAPPENS TO ME?	*James Hadley Chase* 60p
☐	10680 1	KNOCK, KNOCK! WHO'S THERE?	*James Hadley Chase* 60p
☐	10679 8	LAY HER AMONG THE LILIES	*James Hadley Chase* 60p
☐	10616 X	COME EASY, GO EASY	*James Hadley Chase* 65p
☐	10575 9	THE SUCKER PUNCH	*James Hadley Chase* 65p
☐	10574 0	DO ME A FAVOUR: DROP DEAD	*James Hadley Chase* 65p
☐	10522 8	NO ORCHIDS FOR MISS BLANDISH	*James Hadley Chase* 60p
☐	10547 3	BARLOW EXPOSED	*Elwyn Jones* 60p
☐	10338 1	BARLOW COMES TO JUDGEMENT	*Elwyn Jones* 60p
☐	10157 5	DEATH AND BRIGHT WATER	*James Mitchell* 75p
☐	09762 4	RUSSIAN ROULETTE	*James Mitchell* 60p
☐	10636 4	THE EXECUTIONER 28: SAVAGE FIRE	*Don Pendleton* 65p
☐	10635 6	THE EXECUTIONER 27: DIXIE CONVOY	*Don Pendleton* 65p
☐	10617 8	THE DESTROYER 18: FUNNY MONEY	
			Richard Sapir & Warren Murphy 65p
☐	09846 9	THE DESTROYER: TERROR SQUAD	
			Richard Sapir & Warren Murphy 40p
☐	09801 9	THE DESTROYER: MURDER'S SHIELD	
			Richard Sapir & Warren Murphy 40p
☐	09728 4	THE DESTROYER: SUMMIT CHASE	
			Richard Sapir & Warren Murphy 40p
☐	09636 9	THE DESTROYER: UNION BUST	
			Richard Sapir & Warren Murphy 35p
☐	09595 8	THE DESTROYER: DEATH THERAPY	
			Richard Sapir & Warren Murphy 40p
☐	10500 7	THE FRIENDS OF LUCIFER	*Dennis Sinclair* 65p
☐	10353 5	THE BLOOD BROTHERS	*Dennis Sinclair* 60p
☐	10303 9	THE THIRD FORCE	*Dennis Sinclair* 50p
☐	09711 X	THE DEATH DEALERS	*Mickey Spillane* 35p
☐	09710 1	ME, HOOD!	*Mickey Spillane* 35p
☐	09708 X	THE LONG WAIT	*Mickey Spillane* 35p
☐	09577 X	THE LAST COP OUT	*Mickey Spillane* 45p
☐	09111 1	THE ERECTION SET	*Mickey Spillane* 50p
☐	10600 3	OUTSIDER IN AMSTERDAM	*Janwillem van de Wetering* 65p

ORDER FORM

All these books are available at your bookshop or newsagent, or can be ordered direct from the publisher. Just tick the titles you want and fill in the form below.

CORGI BOOKS, Cash Sales Department, P.O. Box 11, Falmouth, Cornwall.

Please send cheque or postal order, no currency.

U.K. send 22p for first book plus 10p per copy for each additional book ordered to a maximum charge of 82p to cover the cost of postage and packing.

B.F.P.O. and Eire allow 22p for first book plus 10p per copy for the next 6 books, and thereafter 4p per book.

Overseas Customers. Please allow 30p for the first book and 10p per copy for each additional book.

NAME (block letters) ....

ADDRESS ....

(JULY 78) ....

While every effort is made to keep prices low, it is sometimes necessary to increase prices at short notice. Corgi books reserve the right to show new retail prices on covers which may differ from those previously advertised in the text or elsewhere.

JILL STEVELY
LYNN DOUGLAS
JANE TISSIMAN
HAZEL PATERSON
FRANCES STUART
LORNA TAYLOR

DENISE
GLAMOUR

39